Savage KISS

A
Beautiful Sinner
Novella

ELENA M. REYES

SUMMARY

There's a shift in the air.

It's pleasant and strumming over my nerve endings as the low clack of heels greets my ears. I don't turn to face her when she's close. Instead, I inhale deeply, and the sweet scent of freesia overtakes my senses. Like a vine wrapping around me, it binds my limbs while I throb for the petite beauty with a hunger that's near maddening.

I want to eat her alive. Consume and gorge myself on what's been denied to me for so long.

My bunny will never leave me again.

CONTENTS

AUTHOR'S NOTE:

This book contains dark elements that some readers might find triggering. This man is brutal and unapologetic, please read at your own discretion.

Contains:

Explicit Violence
Death
Biting & Some Chasing
Drugging
Anal
Obsessive Anti-Hero
Spanking Punishment

ACKNOWLEDGMENTS

This one is for those who love a CRAZY and POSSESSIVE ASF man. Silas King makes no apologies for what he does to reclaim his woman and I find it incredibly sexy. And *sweet* in his own way.

Also, a huge THANK YOU to my readers who've been with me through the good and the bad. I'm humbled by your support and concern for my family. Having you in my corner means the world to me.

And lastly: Lydia, Ana Rita, C.M. Steele, Marti Lynch, Emina; I'M SO THANKFUL FOR YOU. I couldn't do this without your help, push, & love. You guys ROCK!

Hubs, you know the drill. #BBF4LIFE

Playlist

Provenza by Karol G.
River by Bishop Briggs
Love Is A Bitch by Two Feet
Skin by Rihanna
Play With Fire by Sam Tinnesz & Yacht Money
Crazy In Love by Sofia Karlberg
Toxic by 2WEI
Heavy by Linkin Park & Kiiara
Dirty Mind by Boy Epic

Playlist Link: https://spoti.fi/3VpwO5a

1
SILAS

"You touched something that belongs to me."

At the sound of my voice, the man kneeling atop a bed of broken glass shards, naked and bruised, flinches back. Not that he gets far. The click of a gun follows his action, the muzzle pushing deep into the back of his neck while one of *her* guards stands over him.

The woman works with her husband to take care of my most prized possession and is more proficient than her counterpart.

And it's that dedication that brought us to a vacant office building I own not far from the Orlando airport. This was the main office hub for King Aviation a few years ago, but the day I took over, our location moved to a more centralized site.

As did our private jets. From lumped in with commercial flights to a luxury concourse and lucrative agreement with the city politicians—those hungry to stay in a position of control—to an underground network of criminals with ties to my family.

Because money moves people. It creates fear and gives power.

And I provide safe transport to those who are loyal while donating to others who turn a convenient blind eye.

I've also never gotten rid of this place.

To the world, it's our off-hangar storage; completely redone to contain our new prototypes and equipped to run tests from the engineering department. There are guards everywhere. You can only come on site after passing three security checkpoints.

This place is a lie. All lies.

Because every affluent family is full of secrets, and mine is no different.

The heavy metal doors slam shut behind me once I'm fully inside. Their sound is loud, an eerie echo while the other two watch my every move. One with fear. One awaiting orders.

"Please let me go," Boris Nunley whimpers, shifting his position. "This is all a mistake."

I've noticed he's trying to alleviate his left leg, adding more of his weight to the other. The problem with that? He sinks, the glass crunching and slicing the skin there as rivulets continue to drop.

The bloody sight makes me smile, yet it doesn't curb the appetite to slit his throat.

"No. It's not." Taking in the perfect example of human excrement, my eyes narrow while I remove my suit jacket and roll up my sleeves. There's an empty chair not far from where he kneels and I place the garment over the back of it, all the while eyeing my guest. This is the man who didn't take well to the word no. He pushed and taunted my girl—using his status as her direct boss to make her uncomfortable. It happened three times, the first two being verbal invitations to dinner, but after being denied, he grabbed her arm and threatened her job.

Boris didn't get another chance to see her.

Nor will he walk out of this building alive.

That's my secret.

A family legacy.

Sins are paid with blood.

Many have done so in the past, and others will do so in the future. Like the man who's been sitting in his filth for over a month now.

No wife to claim him.

No family to care about his whereabouts.

He's a miserable cunt and will end up dead because of his proclivities. Back in London, he's being dubbed a *no-call, no-show* by the publishing house that employed him. But that's what happens when your bank accounts are empty, your clothing is gone from your flat, and a letter is left behind stating you needed a break and will be on an extended holiday in Peru in search of yourself.

Boris will never return.

I'm owed for his disrespect.

"I'll pay you. My family—"

"You're an orphan who grew up in a nunnery, Mr. Nunley. There is no family or wife, much less children you've claimed as yours. Although, your dark skeletons aren't as hidden as you'd wish." Without giving him a chance to lie, I pulled out a white envelope from my back pocket. It's brimming, unclosed, and I toss the contents at his frame and watch them bounce off his chest and spread about.

Different women. All within the ages of nineteen to twenty-eight, and all have had a bad experience with him of some sort. This behavior stems from his teenage years, unchecked and without consequence, when Boris believed himself invincible. Most of these were verbal attacks—insults and threats—but two allegations have come forward at the publishing house and have been dismissed after citing a misunderstanding.

One of the two is an ex-fling he hit after finding out she was pregnant. Not that he's recognized the child as his, instead claiming it's defamation. That she became obsessed after being turned down.

That was their biggest mistake. Believing a piece of shit without investigating, and more so after only being the head editor for less than a year.

A man like me would never allow his woman out into the world without my protection, known or otherwise. Both her guards have a position at the publishing house: one as security and the other as a personal assistant.

Always watching and reporting back, and when he grabbed her arm, I knew within minutes.

He was taken into custody that night and knocked unconscious for his flight to Florida. One blow to the temple, and he dropped like the utter pussy he is.

"Who are you?" he asks, licking his dry lip and wincing when touching the bloody split in the bottom one. It's a deep cut, too. "I don't know you."

"Willow Caddell."

"What does that prude...*son of a bitch*!" One sharp strike across the bridge of his nose from the guard standing behind him and he shrivels, bowing into himself and then crying out as the glass slices deeper. He tries to jump back and out of the special box of shards made for him, but fails as one of the larger pieces penetrates his right thigh like a stab wound, and when he attempts to remove it, I hold a hand up.

"Leave it."

"Mate, whatever she's told you is a lie." Spit and blood mix on his lip and dribble down the corner, much like the red rivulets of sweat rolling steadily at various areas of his upper body and face. Temple, neck, and chest; all bear the brunt of my guards' wrath. I've yet to touch him, although my hands itch to choke the life out of him. To feel the way his pulse will accelerate, yet the longer I obstruct his airways, it will slow until nothing is left. "I've never come near the insufferable woman."

"Is that so?" Hasn't escaped my notice that he's ignoring the pictures I threw at him.

"Yes."

"Miss Charlotte, if you please."

"With pleasure, sir." She tucks her gun back into its holster and walks over to the coffee bar area I have set up for those working here. It's well stocked with snacks and drinks as well as all their coffee needs, but apart from that, I have a commercial-size tea kettle. It's specially made and is used for anything—from tea to ramen—for large groups at once, but I know this will become my favorite.

Charlotte fills it from the overhead spigot on the wall and flips the switch, the bright orange light on the side coming to life at once. You can hear the heated metal and water begin to sizzle right away. See the steam rise from the spout and billow into the air above while the man whimpers, tries to slither back but can't.

Not when he's tied at the waist to anchors on the cold concrete ground.

Instead, he further drags his already mutilated flesh over the broken glass.

"I didn't touch her." A yell; his body shakes as adrenaline and fear crash into each other. There's also the stench of piss, both old and new, and if I had a weaker stomach, I'd be sick. Then again, there are more bodily fluids than the obvious surrounding him. "She turned me down."

"Uh-huh."

"That girl thinks she's too good for everyone."

"Really?" Charlotte meets my eyes quickly and after my nod, walks off and comes back with a large bottle of vinegar. This takes less than a minute, but enough time for him to see and understand what I'll do with the mixture. "What else did she not do?"

"Please don't."

Taking the steps between us, I drop to his level and meet his panicked stare with my calm one. They say the eyes are the mirror to the soul, and mine are full of hate and thirst for vengeance. He put his hand on her—made my bunny uncomfortable—and his position made him untouchable then.

Not now. Not with me.

"Answer the question." Charlotte walks back over, the boiling mixture now in two regular kettles. "How else did my Willow fail to please you?"

"S-she...*bloody fuck,*" Boris screams out, the pain-filled sound reverberating throughout the spacious room. It echoes and bounces between us, pinging off the walls and then blending with the next cry.

I'm pouring the acidic water at a constant trickle, moving down his chest and abdomen, taking in the way his dermis peels and shrivels in whatever random pattern the water takes. Red welts appear across his pale complexion almost instantly. The damage is gruesome, but I don't stop.

I empty one and toss it aside. The clang of metal is loud and he jumps, spreading his legs a little more. *Perfect.*

The entire content of the other is poured over his small and disgusting dick. Slowly. Steadily. And if his screams were loud before, now they're deafening.

What's left is also a mess; peeling and sliced skin, yet no matter which way he twists and turns, there's no escaping the pain. His agony.

That's when I toss aside the kettle and pick up one of the still-dry pictures. A few remained out of the way, and the woman on it was a thin blonde. "Do you remember her?"

"No." Low. Weak.

"You sure?"

"Yes."

"Fair enough." I place it face up and pick another. "And this one?" Boris shakes his head. "What about this red-haired twenty-something?"

"Please." Blubbering. A bit delirious. His body shudders, the jerky movement of his limbs causing more damage to his mutilated knees. Then there's the slight oozing of the burned flesh. "I-innocent."

"Until proven guilty." I line up the three pictures shown in front of him and then pull out my cell from inside my dress shirt pocket. Two swipes across the screen and I open a folder dedicated to my world and show him the contents. My Willow. My beauty. Every time he approached her, I had proof. Of the incident in question, I have a video.

And I let him watch. Replay it.

Slowly.

"No more."

"I'm going to ask a final question, and I expect honesty. Do you understand?" For a second his eyes roll back, but I'm quicker and land a blow to his midsection, forcing the air from his lungs. The harsh action hurts him but has the desired result and he's awake. "Did you touch Willow Caddell in a menacing nature and with intent to intimidate her?"

"I'm sorry."

"No. You're not." Pocketing my cell, I look him in the eye. For a few seconds, we stay like that, but then my hands are around his neck and I'm squeezing. His eyes flash open in panic, body thrashing in a last attempt to survive, but I tighten my grip and watch as his lips begin to turn a pinkish shade of blue.

The lack of oxygen affects him quickly, his limbs and body becoming heavy, but I don't stop. And as he struggles with his final breaths, I bring my mouth next to his ear. "You were never worthy enough to exist in the same room as her."

It doesn't take long for him to still.

For vacant eyes to stare back at me.

But just to make sure, I snap his neck and let him drop. The world is a better place with him gone, safer for Willow, and I'd move heaven and earth—burn the world to the ground—then build an empire in her name to keep it that way.

All for her. For my heart.

It's time to come home, bunny.

2
SILAS

a drop of condensation rolls down the right side of my beer bottle's neck a week later, meeting with another two near the bottom edge while more begin to form. They race, each gaining speed while those around me continue to discuss some last-minute wedding bullshit I could care less about.

I'm not here to celebrate the happy couple, and the groom knows this.

He owes me his loyalty for more than one reason:

I saved his life. He met his future wife because of me.

Moreover, I was never *his* friend but accepted the man because of his ties to my Willow, not because of whom he's marrying. Yet, he's now someone I value in a different light. He's the means to the end I'm fighting for:

My sweet girl. Always her.

It's always been that way, even if her stubbornness and fear—her doubt in me—kept us apart over the last three years. Since she ran off two days before her college graduation without a single goodbye or explanation, something she'll atone for when the time is right.

Beneath me. Writhing. Giving me what will only ever belong to me.

Because she's stayed single and untouched. I'm her first and last.

During our time apart, I've never taken my eyes off her while she spread her wings professionally, achieving her dream to work for a large publishing company in England. And while the married couple assigned to protect Willow reports daily to confirm this, I trust her. My bunny hasn't entertained a single look or smile from any male; she's faithful to me and the memories we share.

My obsession doesn't blind me; it's simply a motivator. I protect what's mine because many see what I've always known.

She's a gem. Priceless.

And before the end of this trip, I will kill again for the right to her love.

An elbow bumps into my arm, pulling my attention back to the present. "Relax. She'll be here soon."

I don't turn my face toward the voice, knowing it's her cousin and the groom. "When?"

"Her flight should've—"

"It landed thirty minutes ago." Willow arrived in Curacao a little earlier than expected while her guards trailed close enough to keep every other traveler at bay. Unbeknownst to her, they sat in the row across while the rest of the first-class private suites remained empty at my request to the staff.

I own the airline she used. Logged in to her account and switched the flights, booking her on a newer line under King Aviation.

Two other employees followed in a private plane carrying important cargo.

My gift to her. More proof of my love.

"I'm not even going to ask." And I don't reply, just tilt my head to the side a bit and nod for him to carry on, while bringing the bottle to my lips. The cold, hoppy flavor of an island-made IPA is refreshing, and the hint of fruit is pleasant. "Her last text said she's close. I'm sure by now she's here and on her way to freshen up before meeting..." Adam stops, a small chuckle escaping him "...your bored expression tells me you already know this."

I don't confirm but do place my drink down on the high-top table to my right. "She sits beside me tonight and tomorrow."

"Everly sat us by family—"

"She sits beside me, Adam. It's not a request."

"You're making this very hard on me." Now, I meet his eyes. A few beads of sweat dot his brow, and I almost laugh when he runs a nervous hand across the back of his neck. "My fiancée is too smart. She'll know something's up."

"I'm not hiding my intentions. My sister knows why I'm here."

"She does," Everly says then, slipping an arm around her fiancé's waist while the others in the group—the wedding party—walk toward the open-air restaurant where the rehearsal dinner is taking place. Their voices grow dimmer while my sibling smirks at Adam's bewildered expression. "You truly suck at hiding anything."

"How?"

"Honey, I've known this would happen since Silas took a bullet for you. That, and you wrote a note about it on the fridge."

"I did not."

"*Must keep the peace. Silas and Willow.*" His surprise is not at the truth of the statement, but more at how much his wife-to-be knows. Because she's right, and I told him as much when he came to me asking for help; the man is a horrible liar. He flirted with the wrong woman, a married one, and her husband, a low-level shark, wanted retribution over the mistake.

I had the resources to get him out, but not before doing what was needed. The bullet I took was nothing compared to the blood on my hands and my girl's sanity. She loves her family, and as such, he's become a part of those I protect.

And as the owner and CEO of a national airline and multiple properties globally, it was easy.

The right connections make you untouchable. Money is the real power.

That, and my affiliation with multiple criminal enterprises that stem from weapons to drugs—moving a lot of money. Obscene amounts. More than most countries will ever see.

"So you're not upset I'm helping him? During our wedding?"

"You forget he's family."

Adam's eyes narrow a bit, yet he bends his head and lays a tiny kiss on her temple. "You Kings are trouble."

"Yet you decided to attach yourself to one for..." The rest of what Everly says becomes a low hum in the background as there's a shift in the warm air. It's pleasant and strumming over my nerve endings as the low *clack* of heels greets my ears.

I don't turn to face her when she's close. Instead, I inhale deeply, and the sweet scent of freesia overtakes my senses. Like a vine wrapping around me, it binds my limbs while my cock thickens—I throb for the petite beauty with a hunger that's near maddening. Yet I don't move, even if every cell in my body demands that I do.

I want to fucking eat her alive. Consume and gorge myself on what's been denied to me for so long.

Yet outwardly, I remain unaffected. Not when she stops beside me, small hand bumping into mine before reaching forward to wrap her arms around Adam. There's this moment between them, a squeal from her and chuckle from him as the cousins hug tight. And while they reunite, my sister smirks at me.

More than her fiancée, Everly knows what will happen.

My bunny will never escape me again.

"I still can't believe it. You're getting married, Bubba," Willow says, and I nearly groan at the sound. Fuck, that sweet little British accent that seamlessly merges with the Florida girl twang I love will be trouble. *So sexy on her. So dangerous for my sanity.* My beauty is delicious, and I swallow hard. "And to my Everly of all people. How did I miss this?"

"Happy to see you, cousin."

"You left." The to-be-wedded couple answers in unison, a hint of anger in Everly's tone, yet I'll allow it this once. They were close—best friends for years—and she was blindsided too. "That pretty much sums it up, chick."

Stepping out of Adam's embrace, she faces my sister. Face neutral. "How much do you hate me?"

"You're wearing a hot pink dress." Everly's tone barters no argument while mimicking Willow's stance—a characteristic she's picked up from the Kings. Unfazed. No emotion. "Short, puffy, and brighter than anything you've ever seen before."

"Oi, that's cruel." My girl's lip twitches.

"I call it fair." Everly examines her manicured nails.

"And there's no way I can change your mind?"

"No."

Holding a hand out, Willow gives her a sheepish grin. "I'd wear a sack of potatoes if you'd forgive me, Evie. I've missed you."

"Deal. I'll have one made just for you before we leave for our honeymoon," Everly's snark doesn't last more than a few seconds. Then they're hugging and laughing—whispering to each other while I watch. She's ignored my presence, overtaken by the moment, and I've indulged her these few minutes but then Willow pulls back abruptly. Just a bit, enough to fully meet Everly's eyes. "Is something wrong?"

She knows.

I see the small shiver.

The deep inhale and slow exhale.

How her chest expands a second before her head turns and our eyes meet for the first time in three years.

So beautiful. So perfect. So motherfucking mine.

All noise around us ceases, yet her breathing—each accelerated breath—is like a private song meant to hypnotize. I follow the rise and fall of her chest, my eyes taking in the soft curves of each breast in the halter-style romper with a light floral pattern she's wearing and then the long pendant that lies between them.

It's one I know. My last gift to her.

Every woman in my family has eyed the vintage emerald pendant surrounded by diamonds, some even coming right out and asking my father for it, but that piece has always been meant for the woman I marry. The owner demanded it to be that way a year before heart failure took her from us.

My mother died when I was fifteen, and I was old enough then to understand greed and jealousy. I've pissed off many in my quest to make this woman my world—friends and family alike.

Some were successful at hiding this from me; I bought the caring acts, but the scum always rises to the top. True colors can never be hidden for long.

But more importantly, I'm going to end them all.

Every last one who had a hand in our separation.

"Silas." One word. My name.

Motherfuck. A harsh shiver runs through my body, the electrifying satisfaction settling on the tip of my cock and causing a bead of pre-come to roll down the underside. My slacks feel tight, the throb and size of my length unmistakable, and Willow's eyes stray as they've done many times in the past.

It's how we officially met; I purposely bumped into her outside of a lecture hall after a business meeting. Our reactions were immediate. Electricity flowed between us while I gave a hard jerk inside my pants and she gasped, nipples pebbling against the thin cotton of her university shirt. That first touch was all it took—it cemented the emotions growing within me for a while:

This woman was mine.

It made no sense at the time. This sudden compulsion to taste and own a stranger, but I've never questioned it. Not all those years ago. Not today.

Time has proven that she was made from my flesh. Meant to bear my name.

"Willow." It leaves me on a near groan. My tone is tinged with a deep hunger, and Willow's response is one I'm all too familiar with. Those warm eyes close at the sound of my voice and she shivers, goosebumps rising on her fragrant skin. "Long time no see, bunny."

"Christ, help me." Voice low, almost a whisper, she exhales roughly right before flashing the warm browns I've missed, meeting my heated stare. There's a challenge in those orbs—her internal battle—but I won't allow her to fight us ever again.

This dark obsession knows no bounds.

"Don't."

"How have you been, Silas? How's your family?" Bitterness, just a smidge, but I can taste it in her words, in this pathetic attempt to ignore and redirect our conversation. "Are they here already?"

Silly girl, you own me. "Nothing matters but you and me."

"There is no *you and I*." That response makes me chuckle, something that causes Willow to bristle, but before she can try to feed me another lie, I reach out and grip her hip. One sharp tug and she yelps, tripping a bit, but then she's tight against me where she belongs.

Chest to abdomen. Even in her high wedges, my beautiful girl doesn't reach my chin.

Yet, she's exquisite.

The perfect fit for my harsher planes. The soft to my hard.

Another hard flex of my length against her clothed flesh, and she whimpers. It's this minute sound, almost kittenish in its tone, and a smug smile tugs at my lips. I've missed her reactions. How she gasps and moans and is always ready for me.

Moreover, there's no doubt in my mind that if I slip a hand inside her panties, she'll be wet. Soaking through. *Later. Just a little more time.*

Sweeping my lips from the crown of her chestnut hair to her temple, I inhale deep. "I've missed you, Willow. So much."

"Please don't." Yet her fingers are on my shirt, gripping the material tight. Pulling instead of pushing me away while she's against my chest. "We're here for a wedding, and..."

My girl tries to lift her head, but I place a hand at the back of her neck—hold her to me as my cock throbs in time with the heartbeat I feel against my fingertips. The small pulse rises the longer we stay this way, thrumming in a cadence that brings a kind of peace I've been missing since the day she left.

And while her lack of explanation—faith in me—stings, I'll never hold it against her.

It's the others who will pay before we leave this paradise. Their blood will cleanse the wound she left behind.

"They left a while ago. It's just us." Another kiss: this time I lower my lips to the apple of her cheek, nuzzling the warm skin there. "Don't worry about anything but you and me."

"I'm sorry, Silas. There is no us." No real emotions. Just more empty words.

"Are you sure about that?"

"Yes."

Releasing her hip, I pull Willow back by the neck so our eyes meet again, and in them, I find the truth. Hooded, heavy-lidded, and full of lust, I take in the same emotions reflected while her love is hidden behind a poorly erected wall that I vow to destroy.

I'll break her.

I'll accept and welcome what she's kept buried for so long with no judgment.

"Lying doesn't look good on you, bunny."

3

Willow

*B*unny.

My nickname. My lost identity.

A name I thought I'd never hear him call me again, and I can't deny that it fills me with a sense of belonging that's been missing for so long. Maybe it was impulsive of me—a mistake to walk away—but the pain and anguish that tore at my flesh were too much to handle three years ago.

I didn't want to leave him, but the feelings of betrayal wouldn't allow me to see past the pictures in my hands and then accept the consequences after. A threat that led me to board a plane, crying, and then tape those same memories to my London flat's door so I'd never run back to the safety of his arms.

And yet, here I am. I lack the self-control warranted.

Why did I think I could handle this? I'm not ready, yet seeing him was all I've wanted for so long.

Just like this moment has always been inevitable. A written fact in the book of life.

His family is close and loyal to one another, and his sister's wedding is something he—the Kings—would never miss. But more importantly, I came here accepting this truth because when it comes to this man, my control is nearly zilch.

Even while living across the world, I've kept my eyes on his social media and any publication about his business. If he's been seen with anyone. If he's made an appearance at some social event.

I'm a stalker. Obsessed. Ashamed.

Just like Silas knows I'd be here for my cousin, and he'd want answers. Not because of his undying love, but because I walked away from him.

I just thought he'd approach me after. This is too soon.

But then again, Silas King is not a man you ignore and get away with it. He's always been powerful in his own right.

He has to hate me. Has to know what I did.

I left our relationship. I abandoned everything over a manipulation from someone close.

The pictures were a lie—I know that now—but the *after* was life-altering. What I caused is unforgivable, even if it was an accident.

Moreover, I didn't trust him to protect me.

Silas didn't say anything else, and neither did I. Instead, I let the hand on the back of my neck tighten for a few seconds, pin me in place as he's done so many times in the past, and then move to the small of my back. Silently, he brings me into another embrace, and I let him, soaking up what I know will never last before walking toward the noisy restaurant where our families are having dinner.

With every single step closer, I want to run.

Every moment in his presence, my mind replays years of happiness at his side right before the rug was pulled out from under me over another's greed. Because of my stupidity and loss of faith in the man I still love.

I see it all now, and it's a tumultuous torture that pulls a tear from my eye. It rolls down my cheek, curving until it glides into the corner of my mouth before another follows the same path. Then another, and I'm so lost inside the memories I'd trained myself so hard to pretend don't affect me that I don't realize we've stopped.

That his touch is now on my face, forcing me to meet his beautiful blue eyes once again while a scent so purely masculine and *him* overtakes my senses. Warm hands cup my cheeks, thumbs swiping away the evidence of my pain.

"Please don't. I'm standing on a wrathful precipice, sweetheart. Your tears will be their destruction before the timing is right," Silas whispers, and I can taste the ire in those words. Yet, I don't feel them directed at me. Instead, he's begging *me* to be an anchor—to help him control what I'm yet to understand.

I shouldn't have come. I'm not strong enough.

"You would've been back in my arms this week regardless of the location."

"Our story ended." The truth tastes bitter, and I swallow back the small sob building inside my chest. Instead, I cough, pretending that it's just a tickle in the back of my throat while taking a step back, then another. Not that Silas allows me the room; his body is attuned to mine and follows. Not even the shaky hand I hold up to deter him works. "Sometimes people are not meant to be."

"Never." Bending a little further, he places a kiss on the tip of my nose while threading his fingers through mine, bringing my extended hand against his chest. "We've only just begun, bunny."

"Silas, I'm not here to—"

"I've missed the way you say my name." His eyes close for a second, almost as if he needs a moment to gather himself, before flashing open and settling on mine. The fire in them blazes, licking at my every nerve ending, and I can't help but look away.

Shame hits me once again. It's too much.

If he knew what I did...

"Can we go to dinner now?" Voice small, so low, I'm barely heard over the crashing waves not far from where we stand. The tears have ebbed now, his touch more than soothing my distress, but it lingers, and I don't want to be in his presence if I fail. "They're more than likely looking for us."

"In a moment."

"That's not necessary. I'm okay."

"Every lie out of those sweet lips is going to cost you, Willow." Christ, I try. I fight to not react, but a shiver runs through me, and he takes it in. Doesn't miss a single goosebump on my arms or the rapid intake of breath—how I'm helpless against him. "I don't like this new habit of yours, but I'll let it go for now. We have all night to discuss your faults and mine."

"There's nothing to talk about." Weak. Pathetically submissive in tone.

"That's not up for discussion." With the tip of two fingers, Silas swipes across my glossy lips and then lingers where they part. Dipping just the slightest bit. "You're not running away from me again."

"This can't work. We're not the same people."

"I know everything." Ignoring my small gasp, he taps my tongue with the tips of his digits and then pulls back. Expression cooled and body relaxed, Silas is the epitome of arrogant grace with just the right touch of danger. It's what drew me to him; this suave assurance that turned heads while the world bowed at his feet.

He's old-money charm to my upper-middle-class poise.

He's the calm to my raging storm.

I know everything.

That doesn't bring comfort. Not one bit, but when I attempt to move around him and put much-needed distance between us, I find myself off the ground and against a palm tree on my next breath. His hands are on my hips, fingers digging in, yet the sting of his touch causes my nipples to stiffen and my core to flex.

I've always enjoyed him being a little aggressive. Let him control me in bed.

"No. More. Running." Each word is punctuated through clenching teeth, the vein at his neck throbbing while his mouth now hovers over mine. His exhale is my every inhale, and swallowing back a moan becomes nearly painful. My desire for him has never waned and is hard to conceal. "I've let this go on long enough, Willow. It's time to right this wrong."

"What does that even mean?" Breathless. There's also the minute shift of my hips; my pussy clenches in need—searching for what only he can give. Because I could never be with anyone else.

For three years, I've ignored that part of me. The desires that now flame within burn my veins while beads of sweat roll down my back.

European men are attractive and their accents are foreplay to some, but the memory of Silas rendered me immune. No one has caught my attention while I've lived abroad, although more than a few have tried.

Yet each time, the answer was always the same.

No. A resounding no.

Silas has haunted my every waking moment while my dreams are what kept me alive.

I'm ruined. His.

"It means you're mine, bunny." One hand leaves my hip, his body keeping me in place while strong fingers wrap around my throat. They squeeze. Dare me to defy him. "Always have been and always will be." My lips part, words of denial sitting on my tongue, but I'm once again silenced. Silas slams his lips onto mine, and the ferocity takes my breath away just as much as it gives me life.

It's not gentle or sweet. No. The way he slants his mouth over my lips, tongue sliding over mine, pulls a moan from deep within me.

I've missed his savage kiss.

The way he holds me tightly while guiding me to his liking. A rough growl builds in his chest, the sound of pleasure rippling through me, and when I bite his top lip, I'm rewarded by a sharp thrust of his hips.

He's hard. Pulsing.

"More," I whimper, and that's when he pulls back. Right as another rush of wetness ruins the thin fabric that covers where I want him most. "W-what are—"

"Enough."

"But—"

"No, bunny. Not another word." Before I can protest, Silas bites me as I did him before dragging his teeth across the abused flesh. Expression smug, he takes in my flushed cheeks and then lower to my beaded nipples. The sun has begun to set, and there's more than enough natural lighting to see me—my *every* reaction. The truth I can't hide. "Right now, we have a dinner to attend. We will sit and enjoy the time with our family, laugh at whatever stupidity they say, and show them a united front. Do not fight me on this."

His hand remains on my neck, and my lips feel swollen. "Why?"

Why are you doing this? Why do you want to pretend?

"Because your place is by my side." That's it. That's all he says. Silas keeps me at near eye level, our faces close, and had he not been holding me up, I don't think I'd be upright. Because what I see reflected is more than desire and I'm not ready for those emotions.

As is, my knees shake. My body reacts to everything he is:

Male. Handsome. Dominant.

Always sure of himself to the point he's cocky at times, and even that, I find attractive.

This is going to hurt when I'm alone. I shouldn't have let him kiss me.

"The fact you have to ask tells me I've failed you." His voice snaps me out of my self-reproach, but the words cause my heart to clench. This is not his fault. It's all mine.

"You're not responsible for me."

"And that's where you're wrong," he says, voice low. Deep and velvety. "We wouldn't be where we are otherwise." I go to protest and remind him again that I'm single, yet he stops me with a simple shake of his head. "Enough for now. We'll fix this after dinner."

"Maybe it's best if I skip this entire wedding," I mutter, but he hears.

"Keep testing me, Willow." Now his anger is on me. Eyes narrowed, Silas sets me down and steps back, yet I remain in place. "I'm not above punishing you here. Let everyone see you cry for me."

"Don't." In the past, we've played with spanking but never as a discipline. For fun? Yes. Silas knows I like a little pain with my plea-sure, yet the heat in his eyes promises it will hurt. *Maybe that's what I need. To pay for my sins.* "You can't."

"Then be a good girl and take my hand. It's time to face them." That's the choice he gives me, and both will deliver pain. No matter which way I turn, there's no escaping this. Because it's not just him I abandoned. For years, I've hidden behind the guise of work and responsibility. My flesh and blood have traveled to see me, but never the other way around. "Take my hand, bunny. Trust me to protect you."

Against my better judgment, I do just that. Our fingers fit seam-lessly together, intertwined while he brings them to his lips and places a tiny peck across my knuckles. The touch is brief, almost feather-like, but then he's pulling me toward the noisy group cele-brating inside a restaurant not too far away.

If I'm ready or not, it doesn't matter.

He's forcing me to face my fears and the biggest threat to my freedom.

And while I took the risk of being here freely knowing what could happen, I had the safety of Silas's hate to hide behind. After all, *they* wanted me out of the picture.

If I remained unattached to their son, charges wouldn't be pressed against me.

4
Willow

*a*ll noises cease the moment we enter the large, open dining room.

Heads turn our way, and our families wear matching stunned expressions, yet what I see from the to-be-wedded couple is utter relief. Complete and genuine happiness before clinking their glasses together and taking a healthy sip of their wine. And while they seem to celebrate, my mom looks worried while his stepmother appears to have bitten something sour.

From table to table, my eyes bounce around the space, taking in the people I've missed and those I could do with never seeing again. My side of the wedding guest list is small with Adam's parents, a few cousins, and my mom. That's it. Dad died when I was a baby, and it's always been the two of us.

She's dated, but never anyone serious.

Like now. I know she's seeing a surgeon a few years younger than her, but I'm yet to say more than hello to the man over the phone. Maybe someday she'll share, maybe we both will, but I'm more at fault than she is there. I ran and hid instead of facing the consequences.

Instead of seeing the hate or disappointment in Silas's eyes.

Can't escape it now. Not with the way his stepmother's hateful stare bores into me. Her face is pinched tight, the stiff grip she has on her fork an indicator, and yet the man beside her seems calm. Too calm.

Flavio King is a man who demands respect. He's loving to those he considers family and friends, yet I know the other side. I was beneath his outright hostility. Instead, he gave me his back before sending his wife to impart the warning.

More than once, I tried to talk to him. Explain my side.

Yet he denied every attempt at a meeting in those days before I left. He also had his staff refuse my calls, always stating he was busy.

"About time," Flavio says, standing from his chair, and the sound of it scraping against the terracotta flooring is loud. Everyone watches in silence as he makes his way over, hands open wide toward what I assume is his son, but Silas refuses to let me walk away.

I don't want to be near him. Any of them.

"Trust me, bunny." Silas wraps his arm around my waist and tugs me to stand in front of him. Grip tight. Unmovable.

What the hell? "Let me go." Though the words are whispered, they escape through clenching teeth and are delivered with an elbow to his gut. "Don't make me hate you."

"Breathe, baby." That's his response, and it angers me. *Is this his punishment?* "Know that I have you. No one here can hurt you."

"But you?" An angry sound builds in his chest. That stung him, but I'm not given a moment to look back and confirm. Instead, I'm pulled into a hug, fatherly and warm, and this throws me completely off kilter. So much so that my eyes mist and I'm unable to stand my ground.

My arms wrap around the older King, squeezing just as tight.

"I'm sorry, sweet girl. We'll make this right."

"W-what?" I manage past the lump in my throat, unable to control my shaking. "I don't—"

Just like his son, Flavio steps back, releasing me, and then tips my face up with two fingers. Forcing our eyes to meet, and when they do, I don't find disgust in them. No. They hold shame. "You've done nothing wrong, Willow. The blame falls on my family, and those involved will pay." His face shifts before I can say anything, jaw ticking. "Her place is at our table. You both are to my right."

"I'll humor you just this time, old man." No malice. Just mirth in Silas's tone.

"Boss or not, I'm the patriarch."

"I've already established you're old." That makes me snort before I can stop it. They've always thrown barbs at each other. Complete smartasses. "Is something funny, bunny?"

"No. Carry on." They're both looking at me while I retake my place beside Silas; I can feel the stares and look away with heated cheeks. Not that it helps when a second later I have Silas's hand on my back, fingers flexing and his pinky sweeping across the beginning curve of my right asscheek.

He chuckles when I let out a low gasp. "Besides, an angered beast trumps a worried grandpa any day."

"Son, I'm tempted to remind you of how you were conceived. That's a story you've always enjoyed."

"Dear Lord, save me," I mutter under my breath. Everyone is still staring, whispering now while some even point our way. "I'm going to go sit with my mom."

"I'm close to putting you in a home." Silas points at his father before turning his attention back to me and grips the back of my romper, pulling the fabric tight. "And you. Do it, and I'll throw you over my shoulder."

"That's not how this works, Silas."

"It does in my world."

"I've missed this," Flavio says, and my head snaps in his direction. He's grinning, his smile stretching wide while his attention ping-pongs between me and his son. "This is how it should have always been."

That response sits wrong with me.

Angers me, but before I can unleash a bit of the building ire, Silas kisses my temple. The action is simple and sweet and reminds me of our happier times. Of the way he'd do this if I had a migraine or rough day—after bringing me to the edge and then watching me fall helplessly each time we had sex.

At once, I lean back against him and breathe in deep. *I'm fucked. Completely and utterly fucked.*

"Come on, bunny. It's time to be brave." The words are low so only I hear, but to me, they're as if shouted from a rooftop. Clear. Demanding. Leave no way out.

"I don't want to." My tone matches his while I watch his father walk back to his table. Flavio retakes his seat, not sparing his wife a single look, and then waves a waiter over to refill his drink. "This is not my place anymore."

"That's where you're wrong." Turning me before I can protest, Silas bends his head and places a chaste kiss on my lips. The action is quick, causing a few gasps, but none louder than mine. *Why are you doing this to me?* "No more hiding."

Not that I'm given a choice; he takes my hand and gives me a half spin before pulling me behind him. We walk through the diners, some waving hello at us, but he pays them no mind and sits me at the place setting beside his father. Silas takes the seat on my other side.

At once, a glass of white wine is placed in front of me while another waiter sets down a plate with a salad. Silas gets one as well, but there's also a bisque for him with duck breast. The act brings a small smile to my face, and forgetting where I am, I lean over a bit.

"You're the only man I know who would eat soup in this kind of weather."

Those gorgeous blues watch me with amusement. Crinkle a bit at the corner. "It's not the only hot thing I want to devour."

The clearing of a throat brings me to the present and I right myself, embarrassed by my actions. How easily I'm distracted and forget that the enemy surrounds me.

"Nice of you to join us after all this time, Willow. Where have you been hiding?" Calliope King's greeting is as fake as her face. She's had work done, more than the last time we'd been in the same room, and it's not flattering. Not one bit. "Do share with those you abandoned."

"Enough," her husband spits out, cutting her a disapproving look. Also don't miss the way Flavio's hand clenches beside his drink.

"But, darling," high pitched, she exclaims as if offended. "Surely you'd like an explanation too."

"Where she's been is none of your concern." His tone is near acerbic. Cold. This surprises me as Silas's father is a very caring man toward those he loves. He once treated me as a father would his child, but his behavior toward me *after* cut deep. "Remember that."

"It is when your son—"

"Learn your place, Calliope." Silas doesn't say anything else, picking up his spoon to take the first taste of his soup. Immediately he hums in approval and then switches hands, picking up another spoonful and bringing it to my lips while the table now watches in silence. All seats are occupied by their family except one on the other side of the man currently trying to overtake my world again. "Open."

"Are you insane?" I'm shaking my head, moving it away from the raised cutlery. *Why do you keep acting like we're together?* "Stop it."

"Absolutely, and no." Warm fingers grip my thigh and squeeze. His hold is firm. Possessive. "Now open."

"No."

"Now." Not that he gives me another chance to deny him. The warm and perfectly seasoned bisque graces my palette the minute I open my mouth to reject him, pulling a smug grin from Silas. "Delicious, isn't it?"

"Yes." A little breathy. A little turned on. How easily he gets to me is embarrassing.

"See how good it can be when you're not hardheaded." Not a question.

There's a snappy comeback building within. It's right there on the tip of my tongue, but before I can get it out someone slides into the chair beside his. It's a woman. That much I know without looking up as a French-manicured hand lands on his arm holding the cutlery. The way it's placed is dainty, something her perfume isn't, but then her voice greets my ears and my world begins to tumble.

Once again, I'm thrown into my memories.

Same woman. Same shameless way of trying to win his attention.

Then the after. The blood. The pain.

"Silas, sweetheart. Why haven't you come to greet me?" Simpering, Stella Palmer leans closer to him while I'm frozen. All I can do is watch and try to keep my composure. Trying to not fall down the rabbit hole—clawing at my nerves—as *that* night replays like an endless horror reel.

Tears cloud my eyes, making it hard to see through the harsh rain pelting Windemere with a vengeance. It's an expensive area in Orlando where celebrities own homes and the price-per-square-footage makes it impossible for the average person to own property in the more exclusive neighborhoods.

And I just left one of those; one of the many properties the King family owns throughout the state of Florida. I'm angry and want to confront the man who broke my heart, but instead, I dealt with his lover.

After a week apart due to the family business and his responsibilities, I'd come to see him. Brought Silas homemade cookies as a welcome back present after a business trip with his father, but instead of greeting him with open arms, I find myself blocked. Ignored and cast aside.

Something isn't right.

Stella Palmer was on the other side of his gate, smirk in place while my code failed for the third time. Eyes on mine, she pressed something on her visor, and the wrought iron opened painfully slow, and once through, her Mercedes stopped next to my Volkswagen bug.

Her window rolled down; she had in her hand an envelope. "Quit embarrassing yourself, Willow. We're all tired of placating your obsession."

"What the hell are you doing here?"

"Silas isn't one to fuck and tell, sweetheart." With that, she tossed the sealed contents and drove off.

I don't know how long I stayed inside the car. Yet I can recount each painful beat of my heart as picture after picture of them kissing atop a bed filled my hands. Some were clothed. Others were naked, but it was her body the camera was focused on.

The ache I felt was unlike anything I'd ever encountered before. The emptiness was more than I could take, and before rationality could seep through my pain-fueled fog, I reversed and peeled out of his home's entrance.

My foot felt like lead against the pedal. My body was not my own.

"How could you, Silas?" Blinking rapidly, I swallowed back a sob as the stop sign before the main avenue came into view a few minutes later. There wasn't a lot of traffic then, and yet I slowed my car down just the same, knowing that anyone could miss seeing me due to the bad weather. Yet the closer I got; foreboding filled me.

One blink. That's all it took.

Metal screeching slammed into my processor seconds before blinding pain followed. It was loud and it hurt; I could feel the drops of rain and blood landing atop my face along with tiny glass shards cutting into my skin. My head felt woozy, my body not responding no matter how much I wanted to try and sit up.

That's when I realized I was at an odd angle seconds before the other car bursts into flames.

"Leave." Pure, unadulterated anger tinges the one word, and it snaps me back to the present. The force makes me whimper, and the fingers still on my flesh tighten. And for the first time since she sat down, I focused on her face and then his—ping-ponging back and forth while cataloging their expressions.

Hers? The picture of fake innocence.

His? Demonic rage.

But more importantly, I'm confused. Lost. Physically beginning to ache as my ire grows.

"Come now, Silas. There's no need to hide what we—"

"I won't repeat myself, Stella. You will never be welcomed at my table."

5
SILAS

"*She's alive.*" The woman I love has gone deathly still— frozen in place while the viper to my left lets out what she assumes is a cute giggle. Once again Stella's hand smacks mine, playfully trying to get closer while the spoon in my hand bends in half. Grip tight, I destroy the metal before letting it clank inside my near-empty bowl. "She's alive."

My eyes cut to Willow, and I find her emotions fluctuating. Then again, she's always been easy for me to read, and right now, the ire is slowly building. *Good girl. Embrace it.* It's in the tightness of her jaw and the narrowing of her eyes. In the way her fingernails dig into her palm, but before I can reach out and intertwine our fingers, show her I'm here to fix everything, Stella tugs my sleeve.

"How could you bring her here? Hasn't she done..." The words immediately die on her tongue; she shrinks back at the look I give her. This unadulterated fury I've kept a tight leash on for thirty-six fucking months is close to breaking free, the devil in me wanting his pound of flesh. *Blood.* Stella and her accomplice have no idea how fast their clocks are ticking—the time bomb is set to go off before their judge and executioner.

No jury.

Willow is the law, and I'm her enforcer.

But for now, I choose to squeeze Willow's thigh before picking up my glass of water and taking a sip. "Leave."

One word. Five letters, and they drip with my disdain.

Everything they put my girl through will be repaid tenfold.

Just a few more hours.

"Silas," my stepmother interjects after wiping her mouth with the napkin in her lap. Her tone is admonishing. Annoyed. "Don't be rude. She's not the one who deserves this kind of treatment."

"Be thankful we're at my sister's wedding." That's the only warning I give. After tomorrow, it's all fair game.

"Flavio, are you just going to sit there and—"

"Enough." The barked order causes Calliope to snap her lips shut, eyes shifting around the room to see if anyone noticed her husband's reproach. Because that's what matters to people like her: appearances. A gold digger can only hide her true colors for so long. "I won't warn you again. Quit inserting yourself into *my children's* personal affairs."

"Dear, how can you say that?" The fake hurt in her tone does not move a soul at this table. Instead, my father knocks back what's left of his drink. His eyes meet mine after taking in Willow's unmoved form, and with a single nod of his head, I'm given his final decision. Not that it matters to me either way, but I can appreciate the gesture. "I've given my life to this family. Love them as if they were my own."

"See what I mean? You can't turn on your family for her, Silas."

Stella's jealousy drips out of her. It's in every word. She reeks of desperation. "Don't make the same mistake twice."

"Get up and walk out. Last chance," I grit out from between clenched teeth, my jaw ticking. "Now."

"Come on, Silas. There's no need to hide what we—"

"I won't repeat myself, Stella. You will never be welcomed at my table."

Silence. Not a single word from the insipid woman or her puppeteer.

Instead, she's smart enough to stand and quietly slink away like the snake she is, while my stepmother refocuses her attention on the mostly eaten meal in front of her. Sulking, she pushes her vegetables around.

"She's alive, Silas." There's so much hurt in Willow's tone this time, and I find her gorgeous eyes full of unshed tears, searching for answers in mine. In her sad expression, there's pain mixed with regret wrapped in an almost overwhelming bout of anger. "How is she alive?"

Turning in my seat, I push my chair back a bit and lift Willow onto my lap. There's no fight in her when I do, nor is there reproach. Instead, she exhales slowly—each breath dragged out while the stiffness in her limbs becomes pliant the tighter I hold her.

My beautiful, sweet bunny. Motherfucking mine.

Bringing my lips to her ear, I kiss the shell and hold back a grin when she shivers, not giving a single fuck who's watching. "Can you eat for me first, and then I'll explain?"

"You knew?" Now she's accusatory. Willow tries to stand from my lap, but I tighten my arms while nipping her neck. My bite is quick and meant to sting a bit. "Jesus, Silas. Ouch."

"Don't try that again."

"How could you?" The question is meant to be confrontational, but we'll have it out soon enough. We're both at fault here. She'll pay with a red ass, and I'll repent at her pussy one lick at a time. "Why didn't you tell Adam to—"

"I let you live, baby. That's what I did." My words stop her struggles, but before she can ask for an explanation, I stand. There's a small yelp from her; it's barely heard above the noise in the dining room, but I know those in attendance haven't missed a single move. "Now behave. There's a lot to discuss."

"I can walk."

"I'm aware." For the time being, I place her down—give her a false sense of victory in this small battle—yet pull her close. My arm is around her waist, tucking her lithe body against my much harsher planes before addressing those at the table watching. Dad's smirking while Calliope's pinched, overdone face has a forced smile. The other couple sitting with them is unimportant, and up until now, I haven't given them a bit of attention.

We've never been close to her side of the family.

Her brother and his wife are just as entitled. Hypocrites. They've also been wise enough to keep their mouths closed.

"We'll be having dinner in my accommodations."

Dad's smile widens, his eyes crinkling at the corners. "Have a good night, kids."

"We will." I'm walking away before Willow can reply or ask for help. I tug her along and right to the table where my sister and Adam sit. They're at the front of the room and by themselves, something my sister was adamant about.

Yet once we get close, they look up and give us knowing grins, Everly adding a wink. "Already bowing out, big brother?"

"Willow's exhausted after a long day of travel."

"That's understandable." My sister gives me a single nod then. Just like dad's vote. "Want me to send dinner to your place?"

"I'm standing right here." A huff. Snap to her voice. But more importantly, she takes a step closer to my side. Unconscious or not, I love it just the same. "And I can speak for myself, too."

"We know." Leaning down, I place a kiss against her temple. "Doesn't change a thing, though. You're coming with me."

"Only to get answers."

"No, bunny." *Her bravado is adorable.* "You're coming with me because your place has always been at my side."

6

Willow

"*P*lease put me down," I ask for the sixth time, going for the nice approach instead of yelling. Not that it makes a lick of difference to Silas, though, and since leaving the restaurant, it's been this way. I snap and he grunts, but it doesn't change my current predicament.

I'm upside down, watching the tight muscles of his lower back and ass flex with each powerful footfall we take away from those who could help me.

Because Silas barely allowed me to take a few steps on my own the moment we stepped outside and into the warm, late evening breeze. And with my mind clouded—memories and reality slamming into me from all sides—I was powerless to stop him.

37

Not that I want to. Or maybe I should for self-preservation, but seeing him again, being this close, has given me a sense of peace that I've been missing.

That I've craved since the day of the photos and then the horrific crash.

Calliope lied, but who else is involved? Is Silas?

"Relax, Willow. I got you." *Christ.* That tone, so full of hunger, makes me shiver even as a smidge of dread begins to build. For now, I ignore it. Force it back and focus on the pleasure being this close to him brings—like when he threw me over his shoulder as if I weighed nothing at all a few minutes ago.

Then again, compared to him I'm delicate. Tiny.

Silas has always been a force to be reckoned with, and it's more refined now. Gone is the cocky guy I met who knew the world was his for the taking. *No. That's not right.* The man I'm battling against is proud and arrogant, yes, but there's also this aura of danger that exudes from his every pore.

One that calls attention and demands respect, more so than when we were in college.

He's unafraid and sexy. There's a darkness in his eyes, this flash of sin I've noticed a few times now that's new, and it's calling out to me. Wanting something I don't quite understand.

Or maybe I'm seeing things. Wishing for something that's not there to distract me from the predicament I'm in

His disdain and avoidance would've killed me.

His wrath is preferable to my worst fear: being ignored.

I left him over a lie. That hurts and I swallow roughly, eyes stinging as I fight back my unshed tears. Feels as though that's all I've been capable of doing since arriving here. Since taking him in, I've been on a wild rollercoaster of emotions.

One second, I'm desperate and the next, I'm ashamed—a yo-yoing ride that leaves me both breathless and yet full of life.

I truly am his, even if I've lost him.

Silas King is the literal definition of tall, dark, and sexy with clear blue eyes and a sexy grin. At over six foot five and with dark brown hair, he's all muscle and a sharp jaw with just the right amount of stubble that I find arousing.

His hand travels up the back of my bare thigh, fingertips sweeping back and forth just below where the fabric of my jumper ends. The touch is meant to be soothing, but instead, it creates a problem for me.

I'm wet.

Throbbing.

I know what he can do to my body. Have missed it.

"Please be reasonable." Breathless. Can't disguise the need in my voice. "Let me walk."

"No." Fingertips graze just under the edge of my bottoms, right across the crease where thigh and asscheek meet. At once, my legs jump a bit—the flesh he touches squeezing as I feel a small trickle of wetness coat my lace panties.

Thank God no one's here to witness my ragdoll moment.

We're not near the main building anymore or the private cabanas by the shore. No. This brute of a man is heading down a quiet stretch of the walkway before turning left and then right, following a sign that has a large "P" at the center.

"Let's talk like adults. I'm leaving in—"

"Don't, Willow," he growls out, his body tense beneath mine, and then there's a sting. It's loud in the silence of the night, taunting me with its amusement as I whimper in both pain and pleasure. One sharp slap to my backside, and I'm nearly limp in his hold. Then he lands another, same spot, and this time I can't stop a keening sound from escaping. "That's better, bunny. You owe me three years' worth of moans…the sweet way you say my name when you come."

I'm screwed. Is finding out the truth worth this torture? It's not, and the urge to take flight is nearly overwhelming. When it comes to this man there's no fight in me.

I should run back to London.

Away from my endless tormentor.

Because addiction is a scary thing, and Silas is my weakness; a sickness I'll never recover from. I'm always there on the precipice of want and need and a suffocating hunger that brings me to my knees.

The opening and closing of a door bring inside a humid rush of air across my skin and I look up, realizing we're in a large parking garage. My eyes swing from left to right, hoping to catch the attention of anyone that can help—leaving with him will hurt when we go our separate ways—but I find no one.

Not so much as an employee.

God, please help—

But then I'm sliding down his body, strong hands on my hips holding me right where he wants me. Silas pauses my descent when my mound is over his length. His cock gives a few harsh jerks, and I feel it through our clothes as if we were naked and the bulbous tip stroked across my clit.

Electricity pulses through me. Pleasure spreads, but I bite down hard on my bottom lip to keep the moan building at the back of my throat from breaking free.

Everything's moving too fast.

Leave. Stay. I'm confused, yet I don't really want to stop this. I'm afraid to.

Not because I fear him or don't want Silas, but because this might be the last time I see him. Especially if he realizes the kind of woman I've become since leaving. How deeply crazed I am for him.

"Stop that," he snarls, and it's then I notice my back is against a large truck with dark tints in a corner of the lot where visibility is limited. His face is close to mine, our bodies pressed tight, and the thick bulge throbbing against my core is deliciously painful. "You're with me. You are the only person on this island that is safe."

"W-what?" Because what does that even mean? "That makes no sense."

"But it will." Lowering his head, he nips my chin before skimming his mouth lower and toward my pulse point. There, he stops. Kisses the skin, so soft, but then there's a sharp sting and I cry out, the pain startling me. However, there's another problem. I feel it reflected between my legs, the rush of wetness that's sure to be seeping through the thin material covering me. "Fuck, I've missed the heat. The way you're always ready for me."

"I'm not."

"Lie to me again." This time, his teeth dig a little deeper before he licks the abused flesh. "I dare you."

In turn, I choose to not say anything. Blue eyes full of want—anger—challenge me. A few minutes of silence pass between us, stretching to the point I fidget under his penetrating stare, and then, only when he's ready, Silas hums low in satisfaction.

He puts a small bit of space between us right before there's an audible click. The loud beep causes me to jump, a squeak escaping me as I'm pulled a few steps forward before I can question him. Right now, I'm on a tumultuous rollercoaster—more than a bit lost—yet instead, I watch in silence as he reaches past me and grabs the door's handle.

It opens, and his scent, more powerful and concentrated, hits me at once—this naturally earthy tone with just the right hint of citrus that's always made me weak-kneed. Reminds me of all the mornings I'd woken up in his bed during our relationship.

We were never good at keeping our distance.

Needing. Touching. Devouring.

"Get in." Two words, but they're said low and demanding. No mistake. This isn't a request.

"Where are we going?" *I'm in danger. He's going to break me.*

"Get. In." Not that he waits. Silas picks me up before I can take my next breath and I find myself strapped in and with that wicked mouth on mine once more. This kiss is gentle, slow strokes of his tongue and barely there nips before he rakes his teeth across my bottom lip. There's also a small pinch to my bare thigh that feels like the bite of his nail, and I whine into his mouth. "You okay, bunny?"

"Yeah. That just stung a bit."

"I'm sure it did." Something falls by my foot, but I can't look down as it causes a wave of vertigo to hit. Woozy and disoriented, I close my eyes for a second. *What the hell?* "It'll pass in a few hours. You'll be fine."

My door closes then, and Silas makes his way around the car, slipping in behind the wheel before taking the car off idle and into reverse. *When did he start the car?* Not that I'm the most observant right now; all I know and see and understand is him.

But it's always been this way. He's a magnetic pull I've never been able to ignore.

"Fine? What does..." The rest of my sentence is garbled; I suddenly feel drunk. My body is heavy, and the hand I've been rubbing against my leg now flops to the side while panic hits.

"Relax. Just trust me." His voice is soothing in its deep baritone while the cab of the truck sways gently as we make it out of the resort. Each minute that passes, I'm less lucid. So sleepy, and that along with his scent makes me fade in and out. Yet right before it all goes black, I hear him one last time. "I'm never spending a day away from you again, Willow. That's what this all means."

A WHINE ESCAPES me as I'm roused from sleep, and someone chuckles low. The sound is manly, yet far away, and I lazily swat my hand toward the noise to make it stop. *Did I leave the TV on again?* I'm tired and want nothing more than to burrow into these heavenly sheets that smell delicious. However, I don't get far, and my limb is stopped midway, snapping back.

That's not right. Slowly, I'm becoming aware of my surroundings. Of the cool breeze over my naked skin and the sound of crashing waves not far from the room, but what snaps my attention is trying to move my arm again and a hand stopping me. *What the hell?*

"Open your eyes for me, Willow."

"Silas?" I must still be dreaming. Why would he be—?

"I'm here, baby." The words are gentle, yet there's a small bite to them. It's what fully brings me to, and I shiver, the smacking dose of reality taking my breath away. "Look at me."

"No." Instead, I close my eyes tighter and turn my face to the right.

"Don't make me repeat myself, love. You're in enough trouble as it is." A hiss. Low and a bit threatening, yet I don't heed his warning. Not when he shifts and I can feel his body heat above me. Not when everything that's happened since I agreed to be a part of the wedding party flashes through my mind.

Traveling to Curacao.

Seeing Silas.

Him kissing me.

Passing out.

"This is bad?" One tug to each wrist lets me know I'm tied up. Some kind of soft fabric, yet it doesn't budge. I'm also tempted to check my feet, but my heart is racing and fear with a bit of excitement grips me, causing beads of sweat to dot my temples. My skin feels flushed while the last of my drowsiness is replaced by desire. "So bad."

Being with him again is the one thing I've wished for since walking away.

Did it make me a bad person—selfish—that instead of asking to give back the life Calliope made me believe I'd taken, I mourned *him*? She told me it was all my fault. That I was a killer.

To me, it doesn't.

For so long I'd been mad over the pictures and lies, yes, but Stella's life—what I believed was her blood on my hands—had nothing to do with guilt or repentance. My concern was always how *he'd* see me. What crap his family fed him.

"Your first mistake was getting on that plane three years ago." This comes out as a snarl, and involuntarily, my eyes snap to his. Silas is standing above me, bent a bit at the waist while a size thirteen foot is on either side of my body. Another thing that throws me off is I've been sleeping facing up, something I never do. I'm an ass-up and face-to-the-pillow kind of girl. "You left me, Willow."

If he's expecting an answer or apology, I can't at the moment. It's hard to breathe, much less swallow past the current volcanic rush of desire overriding my processors. Overwhelming my senses.

Bad timing? Absolutely.

But this is his fault.

He's all man and rippling muscles—wearing nothing but a pair of low-hung pajama pants—the harsh contours of his six-pack highlighted under the low lighting inside the bedroom we're in while his cock gives a harsh jerk in greeting. Thick. Hard. And my mouth waters.

Then there's the heaving chest, how his hands clench, but he holds back from touching me while I take in a sight, I'd thought I would never see again.

Silas King exudes raw, unadulterated power.

My eyes travel lower as a shaky breath escapes me and I find a few new tattoo additions. Yet, I'm entranced by the largest one. There's a dragon piece across the right side of his body, from hip to shoulder with most of the large head across his pec. Very intricate in its design, I find myself finding little treasures within the larger scales, but it's my initials at the center of its belly that make me gasp.

W. K.

Another reminder of our past. Of how he wanted me to bear his name.

I have the matching letters along with *S. K.* on the inside of each wrist. His are on the left.

Swallowing hard, I once again meet his beautiful blue eyes. They're watching me while his lips curl up at the corner in a way that causes my thighs to clench, an action he doesn't miss.

Silas knows I'm weak for him.

Just like a part of me knew that coming back, there was always a possibility I'd end up under him.

"What now?" I ask, and he doesn't answer at first. No. He lets the minutes pass, each tick of the clock loud inside the room while he devours every single inch of me.

I'm aware that my clothing is missing, and while I should be mad —outraged—there's no anger. No reproach. If anything, there's excitement building. Arousal burns me alive—the wetness on my inner thighs and the tightening of my nipples, the stiff tips throbbing in need of his attention.

Does that make me sick? Maybe. Possibly.

Do I care at this moment? Not one bit.

I'm prepared to accept anything he gives me, and yet, will I survive the after?

His touch. His control. Him.

The temperature rises inside the large bedroom. Sensations weave along my flesh, the most predominant one being need. It's been so long. I've never let another man touch me.

"Now you're going to let me take my pound of flesh, bunny. I want your tears and screams of painful pleasure."

7
SILAS

I know my words scare her, but if there's anyone alive who's safe from me, it's her.

I'm not a perfect man. Never claimed to be. Moreover, I've carried the blood of an enemy on my hands before and will again, but this is something she needs to understand. Willow needs to believe in me—us—and that can only happen after she's atoned for her sins.

And she will.

My girl needs this release. To let it all out until what's left is a beautifully messy doll who lives for me as I breathe for her.

"W-what does that mean, Silas?" Again she tests the restraints, but that gets her nowhere. The silky binds are gentle on her skin yet sturdy and unmoving; she's allowed just enough slack to be comfortable for now, and it can change in the blink of an eye. "Why am I tied up?"

"Because I want you to be." No point in lying.

"That's not a good enough reason." Turning, she tests the right leg first and then the left, grimacing when it stretches the injection site. Both are unattached at the moment and can remain that way, but it's all up to her. "My side hurts, Silas. Why?"

"I know it does." Willow goes from trying to assess why she's sore to looking up at me. Her body's shaking a bit, teeth embedded in her bottom lip, and I won't deny that seeing her at my mercy is a heady concoction. "You left me no choice but to sedate you."

"Are you insane?"

"For you? Yes." No shame. No need to hide it. Dropping to my knees, I straddle her thighs and bring our faces close enough to touch her pouty lips. To nuzzle her jaw and cheek. "But you knew that, love. I've never hidden this."

"We're not those people anymore." Her words are low, but I hear them loud and clear. I also don't miss the way she lifts herself just a bit closer, how she lets out a tiny mewl as I bite down on the flesh just below her left ear. The sting is sharp, yet my bunny doesn't pull away even as the pleasurable sounds coming from her become a small cry. "Christ. Silas!"

"I warned you," I say, bite digging in a little deeper while my cock gives a harsh jerk. I'm throbbing at the mere thought she'll be walking in the wedding tomorrow with my mark of ownership all over her body. "Not another lie."

My hands grip her hips, pinning her in place when she tries weakly to buck me off. No real strength in it. No fire or anger or disgust in her warm orbs. If anything, they're glassy and her pupils are blown wide. *Fucking perfection.* Then I trace each toothy indent with the tip of my tongue, my cock throbbing against the apex of her thighs.

"Let me go." A hiss, but the unmistakable roll of her hips makes me smile.

"No."

"Silas, I'm serious. We can't go down that road again."

"We never had a choice." This time my lips travel from her throat to her mouth, pausing at the corner. "I love you, Willow."

"And you're engraved deep within my soul." Tears build in her eyes, falling out the sides and into the pillow below. The sight cuts me deep. All of this was unnecessary, but life is complicated. She lost her way, but I'll bring her back. Show her the truth she's ignored for so long. "But after everything I've done, how can we work?"

That question comes from trembling lips, lips that I take without hesitation. This time, though, it's slow and sweet, what I've missed about what we were. This tenderness is something that only she can bring out of me. Good or bad, I give her my all.

My right hand leaves her hip and skims low until my fingertips caress her bare mound. She's wet for me. So fucking soft.

And if my words don't sink in, my touch will erase all doubts.

I want her to feel my anger and disappointment.

I want her to accept my love and adoration.

A wanton moan escapes my bunny and I swallow it, sliding my tongue over hers while goosebumps rise across her limbs. There's a shiver and then another roll of the hips, her juices drenching my hand while I run two fingers through her labia. "Oh fuck!"

"So beautiful." Dipping the tip of one digit inside her clenching hole, I pull out and then trace her entrance. Once. Twice. And on the third, I enter knuckle deep, fighting back every instinct that demands I stuff her with my cock and fill her to the brim with my seed. That I breed her until she's round with my child.

We're already married. This would just be the next step.

But not yet. She needs to release all the pain inside.

Roughly, I retake my grip on her sides while ignoring the painful way my balls draw up. Instead, I lift myself before flipping her onto her stomach. The silk ties tug tight for a second and then resettle, hanging a bit on the white sheet. There's no escape for Willow. Not that she's trying.

Instead, she's at my mercy. *Motherfucking mine.*

I've never wanted her complete submission before, but right now I crave it, this volcanic need to show who her master is, annihilating my rationality. That barely-there thread I've been clinging to, but now it's gone, as are my pants. Tossed somewhere I give no fucks about.

Those tears...

I can't accept her pain, more so when she's a victim in this mess. Willow made a mistake by not coming to me, but she did so out of panic. Pure fear that I'd reject her. *Wouldn't even if I could.*

It's why she'll atone, and I'll spoil the fuck out of her after. Today is for both of us.

A small yelp escapes her at the sudden move, but I pay no mind and kneel at the edge of the mattress. Face down and with the tempting curve of her ass on display, I admire her lithe form for a moment. She's all soft, unblemished skin until I reach the small of her back.

There's a tattoo there. One I've never seen nor had any clue about, but fuck, do I approve.

All the King men in my family have one, and mine is across my left shoulder: a crown with a sword going through the top, the stones highlighted in black while the entire piece is surrounded by what is meant to be rays of light. The letter *K* is on the right below the sharp end of the blade.

Hers is just like mine. Down to the most minute detail with the added roses surrounding the crown instead of the highlights.

"Motherfucking beautiful." I run my thumb over the art, admiring each line and the striking contrast between the red of the flowers against the black and white of the rest. "Thank you."

She doesn't respond outside of a shuddering breath and the tiny goosebumps that rise across her flesh. That's all I get from her, and when she turns her head to the right, I notice her closed lids and the small curl at the corner of her lips. So I don't break the trance. Not when I reach over a bit and grab the blindfold placed atop the bedside table, nor when I test the temperature of the warming massage oil I set out earlier.

This room's decorated with her in mind: her pleasure with the right mix of pain. Something she's always enjoyed—that sharp bite and then lasting rush while I take my fill. Today, though, we'll focus a bit more on the latter.

"That feels good," she moans out when I dig my fingertips deeper, running them up and down the center of her back. I'm kneading, working loose some of the tightness in her muscles there. "Don't stop."

"I've never stopped loving you, Willow." My voice carries over her small pants and those asscheeks clench. She's delicate and sweet and mine. Till death and even beyond that, I'll find her in every life. Of that, there is no doubt. "Always will, Mrs. King."

"Silas, I'm—"

"You are." Removing my hand, I ignore her complaint and slip the fabric over her eyes, making sure it's secure before trailing kisses down her spine. She's writhing, and I enjoy the sight. How she arches a bit—as much as the restraints allow—before turning her face in my direction while biting her bottom lip. *Motherfucking tease.* "Now behave."

"You're not letting me go, are you?"

"No." The word hasn't fully left my mouth when I reach over and dip my fingers inside the warming oil. I soak them and catch a little puddle in my palm before dripping it all over her back. There's not an inch of her left untouched. "Never again."

"Oh!" A loud moan. The sound of a happy woman.

Won't last for long. I want her tears before pleasure, and yet I resume my massage techniques from earlier, paying extra attention to her shoulders and neck. She's tense, the knots pronounced, and my cock hardens with every small noise of contentment she emits.

For every moan, a bead or two of pre-come slips from my

engorged head and paints her skin. The pearl-like drops roll down the side of her inner thigh, and fuck, it's a pretty sight. The sudden urge to come all over her is intense, but I rein it in and run both thumbs down her spine.

"Like that, bunny? Feel good?"

"Yes." Throaty. A hint of a mewl. "*Christ,* I needed this."

"Louder." I work my way down her body and don't hold back after I do. My slick hand slides between her legs while adding pressure to the muscle there. The oil and my pre-come mix, seeping into her pores, and I exhale roughly at the intoxicating sight it creates. Willow tenses at that, though, yet after a few seconds—of her own accord—she widens her thighs so beautifully for me.

But it's not enough. It's been too long.

I need more. All of her.

So I kneel between them and spread her until I'm satisfied and her holes, so pretty and pink, contract for me. *Perfection.*

With the tip of two fingers, I trace them. From front to back, I spread her juices and the oil while never penetrating. Just lightly teasing. Counting each time her entrance flexes in search of my fingers or cock.

"Silas, please...please touch me."

"I am touching you." Another slow stroke, this time to her ass, and I give the puckered entrance a light tap with the tip of two drenched digits. "Do you not feel me?"

"Need more." There's a bit of impatience in her tone, and I'm sure a pout on her plump lips.

"How much more?" It's a fair question, yet I can guarantee my limit and hers are very different at the moment. I want more than she's ever given me before. Every. Fucking. Inch. Of. Her. And to prove a point, I slip two fingers knuckle deep inside her cunt before raising my hand high above her right cheek. At the first moan, I bring it down hard and fast, causing Willow to buck on a scream.

That sound. *Christ.*

"Fucking hell, bunny. So sweet," I groan out, watching her writhe and moan. Her body arches into my touch, pussy walls quivering and on the next slap, I pull my fingers out and hold them against her hole. There's no mistaking her cry this time is more pain than pleasure, but we've only just begun.

With my other hand, I remove the blindfold a second before the next two land on the opposite cheek, and at once, blood rushes to the surface. The imprint of my handprint is clear.

"Ouch, Silas! That stung!" She attempts to reach back and soothe her hot skin but meets resistance. The straps keep her in place. *How quickly we forget, bunny.*

That I'm in control.

That I'd always protect her.

My vow two weeks before she ran away.

"Good." With my thumb, I stroke her asshole, pressing a tiny bit deeper with each pass. This she likes, and she undulates while watching me through narrowed eyes. Her head is turned in my direction, lips parted, and soft chestnut curls spread across my bedsheets. The small pants she emits have everything to do with the way I cup her cunt.

Adding pressure. Spreading her wetness.

On her next clench, I enter my thumb to the first knuckle and her rosebud tightens. Clenches so hard, her ass tighter than I remember, but then again years of celibacy will do that to you.

Sure, she has toys.

I have access to her accounts and know her every password.

Those pieces-of-shit vibrators would never be enough, nor is she a fan of the fake. They're a necessity, but knowing her, even those didn't get much use. And the way she's shaking beneath me, trying to shift and penetrate herself deeper, is proof of that.

"Oh my God!" Willow screams out as my free hand lands across her right asscheek and then left, twice in rapid succession while I slip the rest of my finger inside. I hold it there while she bucks and cries out, my name reverberating throughout the room.

Fuck. Closing my eyes for a second, I take in a deep breath and then let it out slowly. My chest expands and a rumbled groan builds, the sight and feel of her has me nearly rabid.

Another strike, and she lifts onto all fours and looks down, her ass swinging left to right and if she'd been standing, I have no doubt she would've been bouncing on the tips of her toes.

"Good girl." Before she can respond, I grab the large pillow beside her body and slide it underneath her hips. "Now behave and take it."

"Please."

"Please what, Willow? Use your words."

8

Willow

$\mathcal{I}$ should be angry, but I'm not.

I should be demanding he stop, but I don't.

Moreover, I regret ever doubting him. Believing that he wouldn't be there for me.

There's this slow rush of warmth spreading through my limbs, and with each strike of his hand—each caress where I need him most —a little of the weight I've been carrying for so long begins to dissipate. It becomes this warm throb that flows from my core to my limbs and then circles around as the next contact with his palm shocks my system.

Does it hurt? Yes.

Do I wish he was buried deep instead? Also, yes.

But I'd take that any day to feeling empty and alone. My soul has craved his touch for so long, and right now, as he spanks me again and then grabs my right cheek, jiggling it a bit, I release a little more of my guilt.

"Tell me, bunny. I need your words."

"More." The word slips past my lips without hesitation. "I need all of you."

"Thank you, love." At once his body's over mine. Silas brings his mouth to my ear, nipping the shell before trailing kisses across my cheek. His exhale is warm. "Now take it like the perfect girl you are."

Not that I'm given a chance to respond, to tell him I'm the thankful one, because on my next intake of breath, the intensity leaves me gasping. There is no reprieve, his hand landing on my flesh with precision, and I cry out with the blow. Then another. Silas doesn't stop, and my skin feels as though it's on fire.

From my butt to the back of my upper thighs, I feel his wrath. His anger is palpable, but there's no hate or reproach, and when he whispers *I love you* on the next strike, a tear slips from my eye. The drop rolls down my left cheek and then disappears into the blankets while another falls. Then another.

I'm unable to contain them and the more my guilt is assuaged, the more they free fall until I'm a sobbing mess. And Silas, that gorgeous man with a huge heart, doesn't stop until he's shown me his emotions through each painful swat, and although the intensity begins to ebb, the latter taps are still raw. A sensual spanking with enough bite to leave me suspended in a state of repentant bliss.

My skin is sensitive and the heat coming off me is palpable, something he enjoys as he grabs an asscheek in each hand and gives a squeeze. A hiss escapes my lips at the action. There's no denying it hurts, but I'm more enraptured by the way he pulls his finger from my back entrance. I've been so lost to his punishment, because there is no other way to explain this, to notice I'd been clenching and unclenching around his digit.

But now I feel it. The rush of wetness that seeps from my core and drips down my thighs—how electrical pulses thrum through me.

However, I'm not given much of a chance to recover or analyze, much less speak, because he's pressed against my back while reaching for something. Sounds like a bowl shifting atop the dresser, but then something wet is brought between our bodies.

His fingers are once again dripping with oil, and he wastes no time in spreading my cheeks. Lips at the back of my neck, he bites down and I roll my hips, an action Silas takes advantage of as he spreads the lubricant over my holes, from front to back, and then dips two fingers inside my ass.

Pumps both in and out. Scissors them until I'm once again gasping, and the roughness of his earlier treatment only adds to the pleasure he's pulling from me. I'm pliant under him. Want this more than anything.

But first, there are words that need to be said. I can't keep them in any longer.

"I'm sorry, Silas."

"I know you are, and that's all in the past now." I feel his lips spread into a grin against my skin, teeth digging in. "But we're not done."

"We're not?" A smile pulls at the corner of my mouth, but I fight it back. The tears haven't ebbed, but that's okay. Let him see another sign of my repentance. "You want more of me?"

"I want it all, Willow." His teeth drag down to my back, then suck the skin there. Hard. "The good. The bad. Your joy and sadness, bunny...every inch of you is mine."

"Is that so?" Turning my head toward him, I push a little against his hold. Savor this bit of playfulness while meeting his heated stare with a lust-filled one of my own. "What makes you so sure?"

"There's been no one else since you left." A shift in his body, and then he's there. His heavy cock slides over each hole, collecting my wetness before mixing it with the oil and his pre-come. Every solid inch is slick, pressing against each entrance and then tapping my clit twice. "Even in death, Mrs. King."

"W-what?" I moan, body seeking him as those words leave me reeling. I'm clenching—flexing each entrance in search of what only he can give me—a distraction from all the questions slamming into my head. The years of pleasure I've denied myself because nothing compares and now, I know he's done the same. *No one else.* "Oh, God."

"Not God, bunny. Say my name."

"Silas."

"Son of a bitch," he hisses, and the hand not gripping his cock grabs my hip and anchors me in place. Can't do anything but take whatever he gifts me. And when I fight the hold, it tightens, pulling a deep and carnal keen from the back of my throat.

My bottom feels hot and raw, but I can't deny that with each pass of his bulbous tip over my puckered hole, I shift as much as I'm allowed toward him. Can't help myself.

I want him. All of him.

Not my fingers. Much less the toys I've spent money on and never opened.

Just need him.

Instinctually, I'm chasing the pain and slight burn I've been without for so long. Because before our separation, we were insatiable. Always willing to try anything once, and anal play was never off the table.

It took a while for me to accept his girth and size. From patience and many attempts to plenty of plugs—from the smallest to largest size—until I was ready. Moreover, the experience was worth it.

There's a level of intimacy that comes from giving yourself that way.

Trust and love and the memory of his guttural grown against my shoulder is something I'll never forget. And I want to relive it. To be his again.

"Please, Silas."

"Fuck, bunny. Say it." Another swipe across, harder this time, and every nerve ending in my body is alight. Shockwaves of pleasure roll through me and settle on my clit; I'm throbbing. Every subtle movement, every rough exhale from him sends me higher.

Yet I need more. So much more.

The pain and pleasure and then his come.

"I love you." Those three words are his undoing. A literal snap of his control and then he's pushing forward, and fuck me, the ardent sensation and his size—just the head—already make me feel split in two.

Silas doesn't stop until he passes the first ring of muscle, his grip on my hip tight. "Are you okay?" I nod, but he doesn't like that, and I'm gifted another spank. Jesus, it hurts. The lash-like sting rushes through me like fire, and I can't stop myself from trying to arch away. Not that I'm allowed. If anything, I'm forced to take another inch. "Tell me, Willow. Don't make me ask you again."

"Yes." A cry. A plea.

"Yes, what?"

"Give me all of you."

"Always, love." His words are punctuated with another small jab, his girth spreading me painfully wide, but I grit my teeth and take it. The ache is there, but it's simultaneously riding the wave with pleasure and they're taking my breath away. "So tight. So mine."

"I was born to be yours."

"Never again," he hisses through clenched teeth, his eyes fixed on my face. "You're never leaving me again. Say it."

"I'm never leaving you again." A whisper. A promise.

"You're my heart." Then he's buried in one smooth stroke to the hilt and holds still. He waits for my body to settle and the burning sensation to turn into a low throb. And when it does and I try to move against him, I'm overtaken by a beast. "Lay there and take me like the perfect girl you are. My girl."

"Silas." That's all I manage to choke out as he pulls out and slides back in. And again. His muscles surround me while the gravelly timbre of his growl vibrates over my skin, grounding me while his thick cock flexes inside of me.

"Fuck, I've missed you." Frantically, I nod at that. There hasn't been a day I haven't mourned what we were, but right now I'm worshiping what he's proving. That I'm his. No matter what. "You belong to me, Willow. Do you understand that?"

"Yes," I hiss through clenched teeth as shivers rock me from head to toe, the sensations so strong I'm crying now for a completely different reason. Two fingers are slipped between me and the pillow, their pressure on my clit causing me to squeeze tight around him. To buck, pulling on the straps still around my wrist so I can reach back and touch him. Because that's what I need.

My fingers over his flesh. To reacquaint myself with every contour and muscle.

"Again, baby. Squeeze a little harder."

"Release me." My demand is met with a hard and punishing thrust that puts me closer to the headboard. A move he follows, pumping into me at a fast pace while I try and get words out. "Let. Go!"

"No."

I'm so close to coming, and all I want is to feel him beneath my fingertips. Need it.

"Please, my king."

"Son of a bitch," Silas snarls out at that. My nickname for him. Because he—that man is my everything. "You dirty girl."

A rush of wetness seeps from me and onto his fingers, fingers he's now lazily stroking my clit with while a loud snap fills the air. This harsh protest of fabric tearing in two a few seconds before I'm pulled up by a hand on my throat, the other rubbing me faster.

Pistoning in and out of me, he takes my ass and rides me without constraint. No break to adjust or take in a much-needed breath. Instead, I'm fucked to a blubbering mess with tears constantly falling down my cheeks and into his hand across my neck. A hand that flexes, tightening a bit before he exhales roughly.

"Come for me, bunny." Pleasure explodes across every nerve ending, yet I manage to reach a hand up and fist his hair—tugging on the silky strands while he brings me to the precipice of pleasure. I'm right there when his harsh breath exhales a low, "Mark your king."

I'm done. Lost.

An almost angry wave of euphoria crests over me, and I lose my senses. Can't make out what he groans from above me, just recognize the vibrations as I pulse and throb and come all over his fingers.

Yet what I'm entranced with is another sensation. Of the way he strokes into me a final time and then the warmth of his come as he fills me to the brim, some leaking out and making a mess below us. And cockily, I can't help but smile—feel proud—with each jerk of his length.

I gave him that.

Only me.

There's been no one else since you left.

Exhaustion settles deep into my bones then, and my eyes close. I can't move even if I tried, and Silas seems to understand this as a second later he drags his cock out and wraps his body around mine. He's warm and strong, and I nestle as close as I can, seconds before it all goes black.

I'm home.

9

SILAS

*S*he's been asleep beside me for a few hours now and the sun is high outside our window. Cozy and warm, Willow's arm is thrown across my abdomen while her leg is on my lower half. Half on me and half on the bed while I twirl a soft lock of chestnut hair around my finger.

Just being. Enjoying the feel of her in my arms once again after so long.

For three years, I've let her live. Peacefully. Carefree.

And while she achieved one of her dreams, I made the moves to ensure her return would be fit for royalty. A queen.

I've been planning our reunion since she left, and it's time for her to accept what we are.

Consumed. Obsessed. Willing to do what is necessary.

The cell phone beside me vibrates, and I grab it with my other hand and end the alarm notification. Everly and Adam's wedding is set to begin in a few hours, late evening, and the stylist will be here to help Willow get ready. Not that she needs it. This girl—my woman—has always been stunning, and the last few years have enhanced her natural perfection.

A low moan escapes her, and I look down after tossing my phone aside. She smiling in her slumber, and the sight is sweet. Her lips are curled at the corners while her eyelids move, dreaming of something that makes her happy. And I hate to disturb her. To end her restful happiness, but today is an important day for us.

Our start. Our revenge.

Turning on my side, I grip her thigh and drape it higher on my hip, opening her to me. Then I wrap my arms around Willow and leave tiny kisses on her fragrant skin, from her hairline to cheek, while my hands explore lower. Down her shoulder and back, to the top of each asscheek, and massage the muscle there. Gently. Careful to not cause her any distress.

A little ass grabbing. A little slip of my fingers over her sensitive holes.

I know she's sore. My bunny winced in her sleep last night when I cleaned her up so it's just a light petting, but it works, and she begins to rouse from her rest just as I dip the tip of a finger into her pussy. She's wet and bare and so fucking soft while I'm hard—throbbing for her.

"Wake up, sweetheart. Today's a big day."

"Don't wanna." There's a pout in her voice, and I bite back a chuckle. I've forgotten how much of a lazy kitten she is and grumpy at times, too. "Comfortable."

"After today, you'll get all the rest you want, bunny."

"I don't sleep well in London." While the words are whispered, Willow is more awake now. Her hips gyrate against my hand, even if it's a slow and deliberate roll of the hips.

"Why?" My thumb rubs tight circles over her clit, and she shivers, head tilting back so our eyes can meet. They're hooded, while those lips are plump and swollen from my earlier abuse. "What do you need?"

"For you to never let me go." So honest. No hesitation.

"That's something you've never had to worry about, Mrs. King." Slipping another finger inside, I curl them forward and press against the rough patch of tissue that causes her eyes to widen and lips to part, a delicious whimper slipping past them. "I've always been there, bunny. I'm never far away."

"Why do you keep calling me...*Silas!*" The fact she's tiny has plenty of advantages in a situation like this one, and I'm lifting her over me within seconds. Hands gripping her hips, I place Willow over my mouth and attach my lips to her clit, flicking the trembling bundle with rough strokes while she holds on to the headboard. "Oh god...I'm—"

"Exquisite." She's wet. Her juices are sweet, and I'm a man possessed as I eat her, quenching my thirst and need. The animal every human has inside, that baser instinct, is beating his chest and demanding more.

Moreover, I take.

Loving her with rough strokes of my tongue and quick nips before slipping two fingers inside again. And when she clenches, thighs shaking on either side of my head, I curl them again and suck where she's most sensitive. Two slow strokes of my digits and she gasps. A single nip to the area above her clit and then drag my teeth over the bundle and she comes.

Tensing and with her mouth open, Willow doesn't make a sound while her hips ride my face. The orgasm slams into her hard, and I eat her through each shake and whimper. Lick every single drop, and when she's trying to pull away from the sensitivity, I bite down on the flesh of her right thigh.

It matches all the others.

Her neck, back, ass, and now thigh are all marked by me. *So beautiful.*

"You're killing me, Silas. I can't..." she pauses, pushing her sweaty hair back from her face while taking in deep breaths "...how am I supposed to walk in the wedding? My body is calling it quits."

"Easy."

At my words, she playfully narrows her eyes while waving a tired hand in the air, asking me to explain. "How so?"

"I'll carry you," I say, ignoring how hard I am. Throbbing and swollen, I can feel beads of pre-come slip from the tip and onto my lower abdomen. Yet I make no move to satiate my needs—this one was for her.

Mine will come tonight.

Atop the grave of our enemies.

"Out of the question." If she was going for climbing off me with grace, Willow fails and instead shimmies down my body and then flops against my chest. "Limping it is today."

"It was never up for discussion."

"Bull..." she trails off after, and I bite back a laugh. Warm brown eyes are staring at her hand, the left one to be precise. Then she's looking at me with a million questions in those expressive orbs, but nothing comes out of those lips that part and close. Her brows are furrowed and her head tilts to the side a bit.

"Ask me."

"What is this?" Shaky. Confused.

"We both know the answer to that question."

"No. I don't."

"You do, love." Pushing away the few strands of hair stuck to her face, I cup her chin and pull her toward me. Poor baby is tired, but she crawls up and stops when our lips hover. Barely touching. "What was my last promise to you, Willow? The exact words."

There's no doubt in my mind she remembers. And I'm proven right when her mouth drops open and her eyes widen. She attempts to sit up, to put distance between us, but I don't allow it and with a hand wrapped around the back of her neck, I pin her in place.

Where she belongs. Her skin on mine. Sharing the same breath.

"How?"

"Answer me. What did I promise you in that voicemail?"

A rough exhale. Body shivering. "That I'd be your wife," she says, so low anyone else would've missed it. Not me. To my ears, it's as if she's screamed the words out, and I smile. Completely at ease. "That one day you'd put a ring on my finger."

"And have I ever lied to you?"

"No."

"Then you have your answer, Mrs. King." My second alarm rings through the room and I reach over, pressing the stop button before resettling with her on my chest. She's still a little tense, maybe a bit in shock, but that too shall pass. Instead, I focus on massaging the area my fingers are cupping—from the base of her skull to her spine —pressing firmly and with slow and measured strokes.

Within minutes, she's pliant again and hums in contentment. "Is this for real?"

"I'd never lie to you, bunny. You've been my wife for three years."

"When?" Still a whisper, but now she's caressing my chest and abdomen, following an invisible path only she's aware of. "How did you—"

"A week after you left," I interrupt, and use the fingers gripping her neck to lift that sweet face. Then I peck her mouth before meeting her stare. I'm letting her see a bit of the darkness I keep hidden. The man who would always protect her. "I've always known where you were and where you worked. When you woke up and went to bed, sweet girl. These last thirty-six months were to give you space while I made the moves necessary to ensure your safety and that of my family. But make no mistake, Willow. You've always come first, and I paid to make it official after your mother gave me her approval. There's a copy of our marriage certificate in my office downstairs if you need to see it."

"I don't understand. You knew?" That's what she paid attention to. There's a hint of hurt in her tone—I knew this would happen, but I'd take it. I'm guilty in this situation, too. My sin was letting them get close enough to harm her. "Why not come to London? Tell me?"

"That Calliope and Stella were stupid enough to cross you? No. Not until after." A rough exhale escapes her at my words, and Willow nods, almost thankful for the answer. "Everything came to light shortly after, the same night I wrecked my house after finding you gone. I'd gone to see my father about taking a leave of absence, but instead, I found him furious while lingering outside of the pool house. We heard it all; their plan, the gloating, and then realized there was a third player involved. It's why I didn't drag you back; finding *him* was too important."

"Why?" Tears of ire build in her eyes, yet they don't fall and I'm so fucking proud of her. This woman is brilliant. Honest. Pure. But more importantly, is owed a blood sacrifice in retribution. "Why did they do this? I deserve to know."

"And you will. I swear this." A final chaste kiss for now, and it's right on time as the doorbell is rung and it chimes throughout the home. Questions linger in her eyes, but I shake my head and her lips purse. "Do you trust me?"

"I do." Not too happy. Annoyed.

"Then it's time to get ready, bunny. The show's about to begin."

Willow makes to move off me; I let her sit up, but that's as far as she gets. Her brows furrow again. "Wait. Why do you have an office in a rental property?"

"Who said it was a rental?" My hands are on her hips, and I move her slick pussy across my cock twice. Just a tease. "This property is yours."

"Mine?"

"Yes. Yours." One last thrust of my hips against her wetness and I turn us and stand from the bed, causing her to yelp. Still in my hold, I wrap her lithe legs around my waist and walk us to the door and through the threshold. There's a large staircase not far from the exit as our suite takes up the entire second floor of the 5500-square-foot home. This overlooks the grand foyer and front door with a peek into one of the three sitting rooms. "I started construction on this property the day after I signed our marriage license, love. My gift to you."

"I wish that you'd come for me." Suddenly, understanding dawns on her expression, and a smirk spreads on her sinful lips. Salacious yet sweet. *All I want to do is bite her again. And again.* "The wedding being here isn't a coincidence, is it? Is this part of our honeymoon, too?"

"In part."

Warm hands cup my cheeks. "Which one?"

"This is the King's apology letter to you."

10
Willow

"Y ou're taking it in stride," Silas notes as we walk hand-in-hand back inside the bedroom a few minutes later, his tone still gravelly from disuse while I'd been asleep. If he closed his eyes or not during that time, I have no clue nor do I ask. All that matters is how content I feel to be back in his arms. With him. Here. "Anything you want to say before I let the hairdresser and makeup artist in?"

"Why wouldn't I be calm, my husband?" *This is real. He's mine.* It comes naturally and tastes like the sweetest dessert. There's also this sense of elation building inside me; it gives me so much pleasure to address him as such, and I also don't miss the way his blue eyes darken. His smile mirrors mine, yet there's still that lingering darkness within that reaches out and tempts me closer. And I find myself wanting to explore it. To see where it takes me. "All I've ever wanted was to be yours, Silas. Anything outside of that is a bonus."

He stops at the edge of the bed and turns, grabbing one of my hands in each of his. His expression is a bit somber, and I don't like it. Hate it. "I robbed you of a wedding, Willow. That's my only regret."

"No, you didn't." Rising onto the tips of my toes, I squish his cheeks and then bite the inside of mine—fight to keep in my amusement at the fishy pout I've created. It never ceases to amaze me how a man so dominant and at times grumpy lets me do as I please with him. Then and now, it seems; a thought that causes me to giggle and for a memory to flash through my mind.

Our last Halloween together and the couple's costume a blow job talked him into.

We were the hottest Joker and Harley Quinn, small booty shorts and all. That's what the oral performance of my life was for; he loved the outfit but hated the looks others gave me.

And more importantly, I enjoyed his possessiveness that night. Multiple times.

I teeter a bit at the image, and his right hand lets go of mine to grab my hip. Steadying me. Heat sweeps across my face and neck, and my giggle turns into a small whimper and those fingers tighten, nails digging in a bit.

"Want to share what has you so flushed?" Voice rough. Deeper. "You went from laughing to blushing. To these perfect little nipples..." with two fingers of his free hand, he tweaks one, a sharp tug that I feel on my clit "...beading for me. Tell me, bunny."

"Not really." My thighs clench, and my head shakes. *I forgot how aroused I always am in his presence. How fast I want to bend over and take him deep, something that in the past made us late to plenty of family dinners or events.* "We need to start getting ready."

Silas raises a challenging brow. "I could always make you."

"You could." Taking a small step back, I ignore the sting this creates on my abused nipple and let my hands fall to his chest while following the contour of his pecs and then six pack. I don't stop until reaching his hard cock and take him in both, tightening my hold and stroking once. *So big. Just a taste, and then run into the bathroom.* "Or would you rather we play a little more?"

"You're going to pay for this." A growl, near angry when the doorbell resonates throughout the home again. Silas slaps my tit once and drops both hands, just watching me from beneath hooded eyes. "That's a promise."

"I'm sure I will at some point." My eyes flick from his throbbing length to his eyes, and I swallow hard. "How bad will it hurt?"

"That's a dangerous game you're playing, Willow."

"I know." Before the last word slips past my lips, I'm dropping to my knees and taking him in my mouth. To the back of my throat and I moan, cheeks hollowing as his taste rocks my senses. It's been too long. I'm deprived, and without a thought to the people waiting outside or to the wedding itself, I stroke what doesn't fit in my mouth while pulling back until just the tip sits on my tongue. A tongue I stick out and show him. How he stretches my lips—the drops leaking from his tip and puddling in my mouth.

"Fuck, beautiful." That's all. He watches, nostrils flaring and hands clenching at his sides. "You look so good with a mouth full of me."

My response is a hum and I skim down again, this time pushing farther than I've ever done so before. His size has always been a bit intimidating, thick and long, but right now I'm determined. *How quickly can I make him come?* Because I want to swallow every drop and taste him in his purest form.

Dropping my hands to his thighs, I go deeper and gag when I'm a little past halfway. My eyes water, my body shaking, but I pause and breathe through my nose while never taking my eyes off him. And it's the sight of him at my mercy, heated blue eyes near glaring, that motivates me.

Hollowing my cheeks, I ignore the door once again and pull back before dropping down again, massaging the underside with my tongue. Silas hisses at that, a guttural *fuck* leaving his lips and I do it again, not stopping until his abs contract and a shiver runs through him.

His scent and body are an aphrodisiac to me, but the way I control him right now is nirvana.

I'm slick and wanting, even after the orgasm he gave me not long ago. But I don't linger or seek a release when I run two fingers through my labia, dipping them inside my entrance to wet them. This is about my needs, yes, but it's the desire to see him come. To watch pleasure sweep through him and savor each drop as it slides down my throat.

I thought I'd never have him like this again. To be his. To have his love.

This is more for me than for him. That hunger has me cupping his balls with wet fingers and tugging—squeezing the swollen sack a little. It's why I fight through my gag reflex and after a few more thrusts, suck him in and then drag his cock out slowly. Linger with just the tip of my tongue caressing the head, breathe in deep, and then force him down to the back of my throat.

"Son of a bitch, beautiful," Silas grits out through clenched teeth as he comes, his jaw so tight it might break while I smile around his length, swallowing every drop I'm gifted. I'm sure I look silly with a mouth stretched wide and a blissed-out expression, but I'm too content to care.

Slowly, I lick him clean while he watches me with a hungry expression, not leaving a single bead of pearl-like fluid behind. When I'm done, I sit back on my knees with a grin. "Much better."

"Get up and on the bed. I want your ass in the—" We're interrupted by his cell phone this time, and he cuts his eyes to the device. Pissed at it. "Run inside the bathroom before I grab you. I'm giving you five seconds."

I don't need to be told twice and run past his grumbling form while grabbing a pair of sweatpants, I'm sure my laughter can be heard throughout the house. There's a lightness in my heart when I step inside the en-suite bath, and when I pause to look at myself in the mirror above the vanity, what I find is someone who's been missing for years...

Me. Happy. Free.

A FEW HOURS LATER, I find myself standing beside Silas at the end of a lit pathway full of rose petals. There's a cool breeze sweeping through us while everyone in attendance stands to watch Everly walk toward her groom. She's smiling so wide while my cousin looks at her with the eyes of a man who would take on the world for her.

I couldn't be happier for them. Love is a beautiful thing, and I'm blessed to have him once again.

It also reminds me of my conversation with my mother earlier. How much her approval put my mind and heart at ease; I need her support now more than ever.

"I've missed seeing you smile, sweetheart," Mom says, walking into the bedroom just as the stylist exits. She's already dressed for the wedding; her long sage dress has an empire waist and then flows straight to the floor. The halter-style top leaves her shoulders and neck bare, something she emphasizes with a chignon hairstyle and compliments with neutral makeup. "Now, come here and give this old woman a hug."

"Old, my butt," I snicker, but then I'm across the room just as quick and wrapping my arms around her waist. At this moment, I'm just a girl who's missed her mom. Who feels the weight of our separation—the guilt of being responsible. "I'm so sorry. I stayed away and—"

"None of that." She's shushing me, rocking us a little while placing a kiss on my forehead. The act is something she's done since I was a kid, and a lone tear escapes from the corner of my eye. Then another. And just like all mothers who seem to know and see it all,

I'm pulled back to meet her now angry stare. "You are not at fault here, kiddo. That Calliope is a bitch and will pay."

Happiness and regret are dominating forces fighting for control over my emotions.

"How much do you know?" I've kept a lot to myself over the years. Tried to shield her from my problems.

"Baby, I wish you would've been more upfront with everything." Taking my hand in hers, she squeezes it and then walks us over to the vanity. Everything I could ever need is there, waiting for me to use, and she picks up a powder brush and sweeps it under each eye, erasing the evidence of my few tears. "I never bought that you were happy there, but I didn't push for answers either, and that's on me. But never again...you hear me? We are a team."

"Yes, ma'am." I give her a mock salute and then she sees it. My ring.

"Good." Smiling a little wider, eyes crinkling at the corner with happiness, she taps my nose with the soft bristles. "Because I don't think that man will ever let you go. He loves you with the same intensity your father loved me, and I'm so blessed to know you'll be taken care of and protected—cherished like the treasure you are."

"Even when I'm being stubborn?"

"Even then, baby girl. Love is tender and kind, but also fierce and unapologetic." Setting the brush down, she cups my face and stares into my eyes. There are tears in hers that don't fall, but I understand. Our family has always been the two of us with a few members we see here or there. However, now that will change. "And when you find it, kid, you hold onto it with both hands and thank God for it every night. You protect and nurture it, but more importantly, you do what's necessary against anyone who wishes to tarnish what you've built. Don't be afraid...be thankful for every single second you're blessed to have him."

"What if what you represent together scares you?" I ask because it's been running through my mind. I love Silas with all that I am, but my anger and volatile thoughts over what his stepmother has done

*worry me. Being in the same room with her—celebrating holidays
and achievements—isn't something I can see myself doing anymore
or ever again.*

I'll never forgive her or Stella.

*Then, there's how easily I accept all he offers and has done
without my consent.*

*I should be running away, yet I can't deny it excites me. The ring
on my left hand is proof of that.*

*"Willow, If something doesn't unhinge you just a smidge or
doesn't add spice to your life, it's not worth doing. Embrace it, and
never run away from it again because life doesn't give you second
chances often."*

"Just a little more, bunny. Be patient." My eyes shift to him, and
I find an indulgent smile. "Trust me, and don't wander off tonight.
Stay by my side."

"Always." No doubt. No hesitation.

Has our story been perfect? No.

Do I wish I'd done things differently? Absolutely.

Because my mother's right, and looking into his eyes, I always
find the answer. We are what's right—what matters—and the
could've, should've, would've don't change a damn thing.

But more importantly, I don't want them to. I'm where I'm
supposed to be and at peace.

So instead, I focus on the happy couple while Silas swipes a
finger across my knuckles. There's no traditional wedding party at
this ceremony, and each couple is divided into groups of three pairs
on either side of the aisle. Some are in a romantic relationship, others
are family, but every person here is basking in the love pouring out
of the soon-to-be newlyweds.

Adam takes Everly's hand from her father and the two exchange
a few words, smiling at each other, and after a nod, the couple turns
to face the officiant. He's an older man, a little portly, and for the life
of me I can't make out a single word he says.

Not when my *husband*—the man I love beyond reason—taps my

wedding ring. I didn't take it off for the event, don't think I ever could, and while I've received more than a few curious looks, it's two sets of eyes in the bride's front row that I'm paying close attention to.

We'll have words before leaving Curacao—of that, there is no doubt—but this time I'm not the young girl they scared off with lies. This version of me is angry. Unable to move past what they did to us.

"...if anyone objects to this union, speak now or forever hold your peace." Every King narrows their eyes toward the guests, me included, and my glare is on Calliope. She's surprised by this; I've never shown animosity before—I was a pushover in the past—but that ended the moment Stella sat down beside Silas yesterday.

Doctored photos are one thing, but to fake Stella's death and make me believe I had blood on my hands...

That's unforgivable.

Without any objection, the priest carries on while Silas moves to stand behind me. He gives me his strength and love while I lean my head back against his chest, watching as his sister and my cousin exchange vows. His hands rub soothing circles on my hips while rings go on their fingers and then he places a gentle kiss on my temple when they share their first as husband and wife.

And when he announces the newlywed couple to the guests, I turn and press my lips to his.

It's my silent promise to stand beside him forever.

My apology for not coming back sooner.

"I know, sweetheart. We have forever now, and that's all that matters."

11

Willow

"You're one persistent pest, Willow. We failed by not killing you in that accident," a feminine voice says from behind me and I turn around, meeting Stella's venomous stare. "But then again, she's always listened to the wrong advice."

"Am I supposed to be afraid?"

"Very." She drops a glass champagne flute on the ground, shattering and spreading sharp shards between us. A few pieces flick off my foot. "Since the moment he brought you home, I knew you'd be an issue. His obsession would be dangerous."

"And yet I feel safe."

"You're not." Overdone lips stretch into a cocky smile while she eyes me from head to toe and back up again. "You'll be of use, though. Broken in hard by the highest bidder and then killed as it's meant to be."

"By you?" I snort. If she's going for threatening, the woman is failing as I watch her with a bored expression. Then again, Stella has never been good at reading the room, and the closer to me she gets, the more I envision my hand striking her face.

"Silly little Willow." Glass crunches beneath her high heels as she takes two steps toward me. Expression gleeful. Disdain drips from her every pore. "You should beg me to spare you."

Why she's here, I still have no clue as Everly never liked her and I'm sure she didn't invite the woman. Yet here she is in a lavender mini dress while I'm taking a breather outside, watching the waves crash on the shore not far from me.

The party inside is winding down and after hours of eating and dancing, I need the quiet. Because like all rollercoasters, I've been going up and up, but the inevitable crash was coming. That plummeting-to-your-death feeling isn't there this time, but exhaustion is, and it's currently fighting the ire within me for a dominating role.

Building to a peak, and I've had to step back from the festivities to make sense of the sudden overload of emotions. From happy to fuming, and in between is this utter feeling of loss that I can't shake off.

Something's missing, and as this woman steps into my personal space, I know what it is clear as day. *I want to choke the life out of her. Make her bleed out as I did when they ripped my heart to pieces.* Broken, I hemorrhaged for years. Barely holding on.

And I want Stella's wounds to be physical. To watch her die.

Maybe I've lost it, too. I'm not a killer.

Yet the desire is there. Can't ignore it.

"I'd be very careful if I were you, Stella." One warning. That's all I'm willing to give her.

"Or what? You think you're protected because he made you his bitch again?" Another step closer, her eyes on the necklace around my neck. The same one she's always envied and when Silas wasn't around, made derogatory comments about how I earned it. "No one can protect you from what's coming, and I'm going to enjoy every moment of your degradation. We're finally going to put the family whore where she belongs."

"Everyone knows you're trash, sweetie. No need to broadcast it," I say, tone even while fingering the jewel that sits between my breasts because I refused to take it off. Don't care if it doesn't pair well with the desert-rose, strapless mermaid scoop dress currently molding to my figure in a way that drove Silas insane all evening. To be honest, I found his huffing and grumbles adorable.

Wonder if he'll punish me for sneaking out. Something I'm not opposed to. His sister dragging him out onto the dance floor is the only reason I was able to step out alone.

"Fuck you."

"No. Thank you."

"I'm going to take everything from you, Willow." Her hand reaches toward my neck, but I don't move. Not when she touches the emerald, and even when she tugs at the chain. Internally, I'm fighting a battle. Trying to hold on to my morals and humanity before I do what every cell in my body begs of me. *I'm going to hurt her. It's inevitable.* "Starting with this necklace. It's going to look so pretty on me while I ride Silas—"

"You have five seconds to remove your hand before I cut it off."

My head snaps in the direction of his voice, and what I find is the devil himself in human form. Silas is glaring at her, right hand inside his dress-pant pocket while two shadows stand not far from him. It's dark out now. The sun has fully set and the moon is high, but when they step closer to where we stand, I know who they are.

What the hell?

Charlotte and her husband, Joe, are close and awaiting orders with the blankest expressions I've ever seen on a person. Almost lifeless, but there's one thing you can't hide and that's disdain, and it shows in their eyes. So much hate, and it's all directed at Stella.

"Silas," she says, a little nervous giggle slipping through, and when I turn to look at her, I find all the bravado gone. My jewelry is released and the woman's gone pallid; a sick part of me rejoices at the sight even if I don't trust this harmless act. "How have you been? You've been ignoring—"

"Cut the shit acting, Stella." His steps come closer, his heat caressing my exposed skin a second before his arm wraps around my midsection. "No one here cares or buys the theatrics."

"I have no idea what you're talking about." A shaky hand runs through her loose blonde waves. "Maybe you should focus on the real enemy here. That woman—"

"Is my wife, Ms. Palmer." Silas lowers his mouth to my temple and lays a tiny kiss there, his voice lower now. Just for me to hear. "You're going to pay for wandering off, bunny. Didn't I tell you to stay near me all day?"

"You did, but it seems I enjoy a little danger."

"Bad girl."

"Maybe."

A huff interrupts our moment; she looks as if she's sucked lemons all night. "She's beneath you, Silas. How could you ruin the bloodline like this?"

Before I can understand what's going on, he's in front of her with his hand around her neck. Squeezing. Lifting her onto the tips of her toes. "You're not worthy of a disease-rotting dick, Stella. Never think you're better than anyone, much less the perfection that is my wife."

"Stop!" She's clawing at his hand, trying to fight his grip, and I don't move a single muscle to help her. Violence isn't something I'd condone in a normal setting, but this is different, and he's being gentle compared to what I wish to do. What I'm going to do given the chance. "Calliope isn't going—"

My husband's chuckle cuts off whatever crap Stella was spewing. "That miserable whore has her own troubles to deal with right now."

"W-what?" She's choking. Face turning red. "What did you do?"

"Be more concerned with what I'm about to do, Ms. Palmer." His back expands and the rippling muscles stretch as he turns her toward Charlotte, who I now realize is next to me. My eyes meet hers for a second and she smiles, giving me a small wink before focusing on Silas once again. "Every sin committed against Willow is going to cost you, stupid girl. I'm going to make you bleed."

With that, he releases her, and she drops to the ground while his eyes are now on mine. Neither of us say a word, watching the other's reaction to what just happened, and I can't stop the small giggle that escapes. Maybe all the pressure and craziness and pain have broken me. Maybe I'm just accepting the inevitable.

Because I don't disagree with his decree.

They all need to pay.

Calliope. Stella. And whoever else is involved.

Those two aren't smart enough to act alone.

"Glen won't allow this." Stella coughs and splutters, eyes bloodshot while trying to fight off Charlotte, who simply yanks her up and then bends her arm uncomfortably behind her back. His fingerprints are also visible on her neck, as is the large dribble of spit that made it onto her dress.

She's a mess. A thought that makes me smile.

"Are you sure about that?" Silas asks, yet gives her his back. Now he's cupping my face, silently asking me if I'm okay. At my nod, he exhales, then tugs me closer. He mouths *they need to pay* before lowering his head to mine and biting my bottom lip "They took you from me, and while I'm not the kind of man who hits a woman, Willow—I can't and won't let that go."

"Do what you must."

"*We* do what we must, baby. Every King will step into the fire when called."

"I'm here with you—"

"He's coming for what's rightfully his, Silas." A desperate shout rings out while Charlotte and her husband move past us, dragging Stella none too gently. "You and that whore will pay for this."

My husband's grin becomes a smirk, an evil glint in his eyes only I see. "Who says he isn't already here?"

AN HOUR LATER, we're outside on the private stretch of beach we own in Curacao. It's late and dark, with strategic lights in place. Moreover, only those who bear the King last name are here to witness Silas's ruling. Flavio, Everly, and Adam—who along with his wife decided to hyphenate his last name with hers so each can carry a piece of their families—stand to the left of a makeshift aisle.

Their expressions are hard. So much hate and anger.

Yet I'm unable to look away from the three individuals kneeling on the wet sand wearing hoods over their heads. I'm riveted by the sight; they're dressed prim and proper with shiny jewelry as they wait for my king. Charlotte and Joe are also mere inches from them, each staring ahead while guns sit inside holsters at their sides.

Two of the individuals I recognize immediately, but who is the man with them? Is this the *Glen* Stella spoke about?

Not that I'm given much time to ponder as Silas walks down the pathway from our home to the beach, bare-chested and with only his slacks on. His expression matches that of the rest of the family. Murderous. So much ire I can almost taste it in the air.

Yet when he looks at me, just a glance, those beautiful blues soften for a second. It's here and then gone, but it gives me the same warm butterflies as the first time we met.

I love you.

As if he heard my thought, Silas smiles. Just for a moment because the second he turns his attention back on the trio, the devil is back.

"Let me go!" Calliope hisses, nails digging into her palms while water laps at her feet. Her long gown with Swarovski crystals is ruined, and the heel of one shoe is broken. "Do you know who I am? What my husband will do to you?"

Silas snaps his fingers, and the hoods are removed from the women. They're frantic, but one more than the other. His stepmother's shocked, to say the least, by those who stand over her, and when she looks over at those kneeling, comprehension dawns across over stretched features.

Pallid. Sweating. She shrinks a bit into herself to appear unthreatening.

But then again, I'd be scared too if Silas looked at me with so much raw fury.

Stella makes an unintelligible noise then and I shift my attention. She's trying to shout, her posture still defiant, but she's barely heard through the duct tape over her lips. And just like her accomplice, her legs are filthy and her makeup undone. Mascara tear tracks run down her cheek, but it's not remorse or worries over her future in that haughty expression.

No. She's still clinging to whatever ideology was drilled into her head. Angry at being subdued.

The third person, though, is silent. Almost unmoving, but the slow and steady rise of his chest tells me he's alive. *Is that Glen?*

"What's the meaning of this, Silas? How can you—" Calliope's cut off by a single strike from Everly across her face, causing her to scream. Open palm, my sister-in-law's blow snaps her head to the side, and nearly topples the older woman who catches herself by digging her French manicured nails into the sand. "Why?"

"Speak when spoken to, *Mother.*" The words are sneered with so much animosity in each syllable. Moreover, my sister-in-law has never used the term when addressing or speaking to the woman her father married. "Isn't that the first lesson in becoming a man's arm candy?"

"Flavio, please don't just stand there. Look at how they treat me."

"You spent years trying to teach me—pair me with whom you deemed worthy," the two women speak in unison. In the end, though, Everly chuckles while her father remains impassive. He's unmoved, yet there's a tick in his jaw. Palpable anger like his son. "Not that you've ever been anything more than a cheap imitation of what you aspired to be."

"Don't ever compare me to that—" Calliope doesn't get to finish. This time she ends up with a face full of sand after Everly kicks her in the mouth with the pair of white heels she wore to her wedding. Then she slips them off, and like me, stands barefoot. It's also now that I notice her dress is a sexy copy of her wedding gown, just shorter and with a lot less lace. Tight, strapless, and instead of flowing out into a tulle A-line skirt, its bodice is more bodycon styled.

"You never did learn your place, did you?" Silas drops down to her level, his expression mocking. "But then again, that's always been your problem, Calliope. Always wanting more. Thinking yourself above the hand that feeds."

"I am better." Once again, her voice is low, yet we all heard her.

"Silly old woman." I take note of the handkerchief in his hand, not knowing where it came from, and watch him toss it at her. The material bounces off her forehead, catching a little blood from her eyebrow before flowing to the ground. "You were born nothing and will die with nothing."

12

Willow

$\mathscr{H}$is eyes flash to Joe, who reaches down and with a quick snatch of his hand removes Stella's duct tape. At once she screams, and the shrill sound causes my lips to twitch. I'm amused by this display—feel a little vindication in her pain—and then just as quickly, I question my sanity.

How can I enjoy this? Why am I not putting a stop to this?

Yet, I feel my heart pitter patter at the sight of him so dominant and in control.

Something must be wrong with me.

Do I want vengeance? Yes, but how far am I willing to go for it?

"You're making a grave mistake, Silas. Stop this before it's too late." Gone is Calliope's polished demeanor and she spits on the ground, trying to clear some of the blood out of her mouth. His sister did land a good solid kick. "You belong with someone like Stella. Do the right thing. Let us go and marry her before I end you all."

"Your threats amuse me." Charlotte does the honors this time and removes the last hood and the two women gasp, nearly in tears at the sight of a man I've seen once or twice before. His face is swollen, and dry rivulets of his life's essence leave behind a pattern that depicts true brutality. From his left eye—which is nearly shut—to his chin, he's marked by cuts and bruises, and the worst of it is on his throat.

As if he'd been tied by the neck and whatever material used had dug in, tearing flesh in a horrific pattern. It takes me a moment, to see past the ugly to realize why he's familiar, but then it hits.

"I met him in London." The words leave me before I realize it, and all heads snap in my direction. Yet, the eyes I focus on are my husband's. "He was in a meeting with my boss a few months ago; we didn't speak, but I avoided him just the same."

"Why is that?" Silas asks, tone gentle and expression soft while standing to full height. He doesn't come closer. Instead, he moves a few paces back before crossing his arms over his chest. "Did he do something I'm unaware of? Did he touch you?"

His question is for me, but I don't miss the harsh cut of his eyes toward the couple who up until an hour ago were nothing more than coworkers—something else I haven't fully digested.

I should be mad. Furious he had people following me, but once again my traitorous heart thumps in glee at the fact. *He loves me just as madly as I do him.* And I think it's because of *that* I'm accepting of *this*. Why I'm not running away from the crimes being committed before me.

I will love him through the good and the bad. Never judge. Never abandon again.

"Bunny, did he put his hands on you?"

That question pulls me from my thoughts. "No, babe. He never got close, just gave me a bad vibe and I took heed."

"Good girl." *Christ.* That praise makes me smile. Worst moment to, I know this, but I also can't stop myself. Not when his blue eyes become heated, raking me over from head to toe and back up again. "And when was the second time?"

"Last year's office Christmas party."

"Understood." That's it. As if it all makes sense. Refocusing his attention on the women, he waves a hand over to the beaten man. "So this is your savior? Who I should fear?"

"Hurting him will be your—" Calliope abruptly stops, her entire body shaking as if in immense pain. *What is he to her?*

"Finish your sentence." Silence from her while Stella cries; the sound would be gut-wrenching if I didn't abhor the woman. "Tell us. Who is he to you?"

"You'll die for this." Stella wipes at her cheeks, chest heaving while a hand reaches out toward the man. At first, he startles at the touch, a hoarse, painful sound coming from the back of his throat and that adds to her distress. *She's acting like a woman in love.* "You have nothing and no one, Silas. You'll soon come to understand this."

His snort is nothing but condescending. "Please don't keep us in this anticipation. Who exactly should I fear?"

"Me." For a beat after her response there's silence, but then my husband laughs. Loud. Boisterous. The others do, too, but I'm riveted by the scene in front of me: his mocking and her anger. *I'm missing something here.* "Code red."

Nothing.

No one moves.

Taking it upon himself, Silas snaps his fingers once. Then, we're surrounded. Men and women in dark clothing, some with masks on their faces, stand with high-caliber weapons pointed at the man in question.

"That's how it works, Stella. Loyalty."

"The fuck!" she screeches while Calliope is silently pinging her attention from her husband to his son, trying to find a way out without drawing attention. "I've paid you generously to protect me and end him. I want Silas on his knees now…kill the useless stain he brought home."

Stella's words—the way her eyes veer toward me with contempt remind me of one of the worst moments of my life. I'm slammed into another memory. Another place and time where I falsely believed Calliope cared and was worried for me before uttering those same words:

Useless. Stain.

"You're an embarrassment, Willow. Look at what you've done," Silas's stepmother says, tone full of disgust while entering my apart- ment a few days after the crash. *"A useless stain. A murderer."*

"Calliope, how can you say that?" Tears immediately brim my eyes, hurt filling my bruised chest. *"You know I'd never hurt anyone on purpose."*

"And yet you killed her." She doesn't ask me for my version of the story. Doesn't care about me one bit, and it's never been more obvious.

I'm aching and bruised all along my face, arm, and ribs—have stitches across my hand from an embedded glass shard—and yet this is what she came for? To insult me?

They've ignored me for days.

Silas hasn't come either.

Voicemails to him and his father have gone ignored, and no one at their office will let me in to see the older King. Because if anyone can help me, it's him. He claimed time and time again that I'd become like a daughter to him, and now I'm in trouble.

Legally, it was an accident. Bad timing and weather caused the crash and the more I think about it, I can't help but feel something's wrong. How can I be held responsible when I'd been slowing down before reaching the stop sign? When Stella's car hit me.

Instead, I've been blacklisted. Abandoned. Forgotten.

Where are you, Silas? I need you.

"I think you should leave."

"My son made a mistake with you. We all did." Suddenly, pain explodes across my face and my head snaps to the side. I can feel the sting where each finger made contact with my cheek. *"You hurt my daughter, Willow. I'm going to end you for this."*

"What the hell are you talking about?" Cupping my cheek, I watch her through watery eyes and take in the hate staring back at me—the disgust—and it cuts deep. While we've never been best friends, our relationship has always been comfortable and quiet; I'm at ease in her presence. Or was. *"What have I done to you?"*

"Merely exist." Calliope moves to walk further into the living room of my modest one-bedroom, but I block her. *"Move."*

"Leave."

"You've always been an insolent little bitch, and it's going to cost you everything." The smile on her face is near gleeful, Calliope is loving this moment, and my chest caves in a little more. *"Run, Willow. Leave this country and never come back, because if you think I'm your worst enemy, you have no idea what Silas is capable of."*

"Silas knows?" Voice small, helpless, while I grip onto the door-frame as my knees go weak. I'm standing, but don't know for how much longer. *"He hates me?"*

"He will. Just like there will be cops knocking on your door soon enough if you don't run."

"She's your daughter."

The moment those words leave me, everything stills and silence ensues. Yet I'm looking at Calliope as a whooshing sound reverberates through my skull, growing in tempo while a throb builds in my muscles—the kind of hurt I'll never forget.

I'm taken back to the crash and the pain that followed, the lashes of anguish while bruises healed and then stitches were removed. Those headaches that are common now after slamming my head against the driver-side door while shards dug into my skin and my blood seeped from the wounds. The months in isolation after fleeing to London and the nights spent crying myself to sleep because all I wanted was to be home.

Here. With my family. *With Silas.*

It's all here with me as this living, breathing pulse that grows and overtakes my rationality.

Hate: one word with four letters. A complex emotion, yet it's simple to detect and melds with each molecule in my DNA until I'm no longer thinking clearly.

That's what's festering. Thumping inside my chest.

I'm owed, and I want my payment.

"You took everything from me for her. Didn't you, Calliope?" A mirthless laugh escapes me while the two women, kneeling and looking down, lean back as I pace forward. While the younger of the two shifts closer to the beaten man that flinches at any contact. "All for her. For the ungrateful bitch you spawned who threw a tantrum because what she wanted wasn't hers to have. What she only wants for greed-filled reasons."

Silence. No denial or confirmation of the fact.

"You'd do well to answer her, S*tepmother*. My wife holds your lives in the palm of her tiny hands."

"I think we should all sit and talk this out, Silas." Still doesn't answer or look at me. Her focus is now on my husband—he, she will respond to—and I take it for the disrespect it is. As if doing so is beneath her. "No need for any more violence. Your family has done enough."

"That's where you're wrong. We've only just begun."

There's no rhyme or reason to what happens next, but I cut my eyes to Charlotte and point. Her reaction is instant, the loud gunshot rifling through the air and meeting its target before my next intake of breath. Then there's a cry—the sound loud and full of pain, but I'm not moved by it.

If anything, I want to hear it again. And again.

"Stop!" Calliope yells out before throwing her body over Stella's. When she looks back at me, I have all the confirmation I need, but it's not enough. She owes me the verbal. "Don't hurt them."

"Then answer my questions."

"Yes." Low. Very low.

"Louder so everyone can hear you."

Calliope grits her teeth at my command while her hands add pressure to the wound on Stella's thigh. It won't kill her unless she doesn't get attention and bleeds out slowly, but the large gauge of Charlotte's gun left a sizable hole that could cause severe damage.

At the very least, she'll be walking with a limp for the rest of her life.

I want her dead. The weight of that thought shakes me to my core, but not because it's untrue. There's a difference between wishing harm and causing it, and I want the latter. Can no longer deny it, and more so as I tilt my head and shift my eyes to Silas and catch the handsome grin on his face.

He looks proud of me. So much love in that heated stare, and my heart flutters again.

"You're all insane and will rot in jail for the rest of your lives," Calliope grits out, her fingers soaked while the bleeding woman starts to shake. Adrenaline is crashing through her—the shock and pain leave her gasping for breath. "I'm going to—"

"Stella is her daughter." All heads snap toward the weak man, his head turned in their direction, squinting through his swollen eyes. In his tone, I catch fear and frustration, but also a tinge of anger. "We're all related."

"Interesting."

"Shut up!" Stella hisses, trying to push her mother away while the other maintains position—using the dirty train of her gown to try and contain the sanguine gush. "How can you just sit there and do nothing? How can you let them hurt me?"

"Because I never loved you." As he speaks, his split lip tears again, his mouth and teeth becoming red. Then there's the clench of his hands, how he tries to glare at the pair, but it hurts and instead he looks at me. "Calliope is my stepmother from a previous marriage, and after my father died, she continued to be my guardian."

"And Stella is also...?" *Did the Kings know?*

"No." Glen shakes his head, then grimaces. "She's her biological daughter and was kept hidden."

"For God's sake, Glen. Be quiet," the older of the two women demands, body language stiff and face pinched tight. "Not another word."

"Fuck you both. You got me into this mess."

Before he can respond, Flavio, who's been silent, whistles sharply. All attention diverts to him. "Why, Glen? I treated you as family."

"You knew about him?" I ask, yet every member except Adam and me nods. There was never a picture of him on the walls or mantle. "Why was he never around? No one ever mentioned him."

"He chose to stay hidden and work at the Chicago office for King Aviation. This was before you came into the picture, and he always had an excuse for staying away. For years, I thought he'd found someone there." Flavio purses his lips, disappointment clear in his expression. "Glen said he wanted to make a name for himself and not fall under Silas's shadow, something I respected." His exhale is loud before shaking his head. "You disappoint me, kid."

"I know."

"Then why betray us?"

Glen shrugs, yet the move is far from nonchalant. It's more resigned. "Calliope made me an offer too good to pass up. No one would."

"Glen, shut the fuck up!" Stella shifts a bit, dragging her bleeding leg so she can face him, but the cock of a gun makes her pause. Her eyes dart between Charlotte and Glen—her hand reaching out for him—but he denies her touch as if burned. "Baby, please. Be the man I know you are and end this. They work for you, not the Kings."

What in the ever-loving crap is she on about?

"Tell her, Glen." Silas takes the few steps separating them and grips the man's face harshly, causing him to cry out. "Tell her the truth."

"I was going to kill you after."

13
SILAS

The expressions on both mother and daughter is priceless.

Anguish. Anger. Unable to comprehend how something so poorly thought out could end up so wrong, but then again, that's the problem with greed. People become comfortable within their obsession to conquer and take, but the attached consequences don't compute within the simplest of minds.

They lose sight of the real danger: someone like me.

And we exist all over the world with varying levels of evil within our souls.

Because greed will blind you and then get you killed.

Ambition will be the one planning to become a killer.

"You can't mean that," Stella whimpers, trying to grab his hand, but Glen simply scoffs and then spits on the sand between them. "We're family. Please remember."

"I do." He looks at her as if she was shit on the bottom of his shoe "…I loathe you both."

He was delivered to the island thirty minutes after Willow arrived and via the two guards standing behind my family. No bruises or cuts; I delivered those myself while my beauty rested—slept off the effects of the drugs—after carrying her over the threshold yesterday.

"Get up." The spat words reverberate throughout the small basement of our vacation home. There's nothing here but four cement walls, one small window high above where my guest could reach, and metal chains embedded deep into the cement. And that's where he is.

Glen Silver is the son of a failed businessman whose mother died while he was young. An orphan at the age of four, his father didn't stay single for long and a year after becoming a widow, he made Calliope his wife after she bent over at his whim a few times. Neither of the two was smart enough to lift a failed restaurant—Silver had four fast-food franchises go bankrupt before his un-investigated death—yet the pair thought highly of themselves.

Stella, though, comes from a one-night stand with a married senator two years after her husband's death. The politician never gave either of them the time of day. Financially, he paid them off to remain a dirty secret, but that's all she'll ever be. Unwanted and with a mother who hid her out of convenience and who manipulated her every move.

"Silas, what's the meaning of this? Why the fuck am I chained?" he says quickly, jerking up while the metal keeping him in place rattles. They clank and groan at the sudden movement, ruthlessly pulling him back as his slack is almost nonexistent. "Let me out."

"Of course." There's only one guard inside the room with me and after I nod, Glen falls to the floor while rubbing his wrist. "Anything else I can do for you? Anything to make you more comfortable?"

"I demand to know why I'm here!" His raised voice makes my

employee punch Glen without my permission, yet I forgive him imme-diately.

"Get out and lock the door. I'll knock when I'm ready."

"Yes, sir."

The moment the heavy metal door closes, I strike. The first punch throws him back, head banging against the rough cinderblock. This is the one space in the home I purposely left unfinished, yet the soundproofing is immaculate. No one will disturb my wife.

"Get the fuck up," I snarl, lip curling up in disgust when he cups the side of his face, whimpering at the broken skin.

"Why are you doing this? My mother won't—"

He's cut off by my hand gripping his hair, forcing his neck to arch in an uncomfortable direction. "That bitch is the reason you're here, Glen. Or did you think me so stupid as to not know what you're all after?"

"Whatever this is, it's a mistake. Silas, we're family." Blunt fingernails try to dig into my wrist, pulling and yanking to be released, but I use my grip to bring him down toward my raised knee. Once. Twice. Three times, and I'm satisfied when a gash opens across the bridge of his nose and then the crunch of his nasal bone accompanies it. Blood pours from the wound, staining my dress pants, and I pat his cheek.

"You are no family of mine, Glen." Near the window's ledge, there's a set of brass knuckles and I pick them up, sliding my fingers through each hole. Each digit squeezes tight and then unclenches; I've played nice long enough—gave the man chance after chance to not follow down the path of destruction. "What you are is an egotis-tical son of a bitch with ideas of grandeur far exceeding what you truly are—just like your father."

"Fuck you." Red spittle flies from his mouth. His eyes are begin-ning to close a bit as the damage to his nose begins to swell. "I'm nothing like that bastard. Your whore, though—"

I smile when the metal breaks through the flesh of his cheek, then again when his tooth falls out on the next blow. Yet I don't stop. Not when he cries or when he pleads. Instead, I punch him again before knocking him almost unconscious when I direct my strength to his neck.

He lands on the floor, back facing up, and I straddle his chest. The burn in my arms feels good, more so when his head bounces off the cold floor and rivulets of red spread around us. Not that I stop. No. I beat the shit out of him until his words are garbled and his bloodied face is near unrecognizable.

Then I pat his cheek, spreading the red liquid across his cheekbones and down to his mouth where I place the metal. "Kiss it."

"Please stop." His garbled response incenses me.

"Did you ever care about Willow's well-being?" Glen tries to respond, but can't with my other hand around his neck, holding tight. Instead, he coughs and fights for his next breath while I push the brass knuckles in my other hand deeper into his mouth. There's a gag and then tears, but neither moves me. "You were going to take, abuse, and then sell her to the highest bidder with the help of her boss. You wanted her broken as did Calliope and Stella, yet the latter hates your obsession with my wife."

"Stop. Can't breathe!" A whisper-shout is all he can manage around the oral intrusion, near passing out. "No—"

"You fucked with the wrong man, Glen. That woman is my life."

His chest heaves a final time, body stilling, and I release him. Leave him on the floor for my guard to shackle.

This isn't the end...yet.

A laugh comes from my wife, and I bite the inside of my cheek to not join her. Willow's enjoying this, wiping a stray tear from the corner of her eye while everything she's run from hits her. The reality of what they did.

The time we lost.

"You miserable, sick assholes." Her attention bounces between the three but lingers on Stella the longest. A flash of darkness flits across her expression, but then the amusement is back. "All of this for nothing. You love him, yet he hates you."

"I'm going to kill you myself." Stella's threat falls flat when the man beside her snorts through his injuries. That pains her and the idiot's bottom lip trembles; her watery eyes turn toward him. "Baby, you promised. I gave you everything, every piece of me," she whispers the last part low, "and you vowed—swore—I'd always be yours. That we were in this together."

"You were nothing more than an easy lay I could manipulate." He shrugs. A little grimace after. "You're spoiled and narcissistic, Stella. A few quick fucks and some lies had you eating out of the palm of my hand."

"Please, don't." The way she reacts is as if he struck her. She recoils, tears running down her cheeks while her chest caves. "It's not too late to fix whatever's happening here. Remember our plans, baby. We're so close to the money and power."

"All I ask is that you kill them before me."

She tries to lunge for him, but then screams as the action tweaks her bullet hole. Her mother watches them, but what I find interesting is how she's trying to inch away now. While her daughter and stepson speak, Calliope stops putting pressure on the wound and shifts over a few paces.

It's hard, but I hold in my amusement.

Willow doesn't, though. There's a hint of depravity in her eyes that causes me to shiver. The electrifying sensation runs down my spine while I watch her crook a finger at Charlotte. The guard moves toward her while her husband adjusts his position, his gun aimed at Calliope now.

I'm not the only one who noticed her move.

Charlotte leans in close and they exchange words, and I'm pleasantly surprised when she hands her Glock to my bunny. No hesitation.

Willow checks the safety immediately, something she learned to do after visiting the shooting range near our Orlando home, and then walks toward me.

Each sway of her hips makes my mouth water.

Her hold on the gun makes my cock hard.

They have no idea just how good her aim is. Almost as good as mine; I've enjoyed her challenges while at the range or our backyard. Our land is large enough to have a little setup for talking smack, shooting targets, and then bending her over.

"How mad would you be if I handled this?" My response is to bring a hand to her neck, gripping tightly as I lower my lips to hers. This isn't gentle or sweet; I claim her mouth unapologetically—my hunger for her is animalistic.

Our tongues clash and teeth nip; I groan loudly while a keening, adorable mewl slips from her. The harshness of the gun between our bodies—against her chest and my stomach—while she strokes the planes of my abdomen with soft fingertips. So dangerous. Could be stupid.

And yet, I jerk harshly behind the zipper of my pants while her nipples bead.

"Do whatever you want, love. Doesn't matter to me." Another slide of my tongue across hers, savoring her sweet taste along with the hint of wine she'd had earlier. "All I care about is the night ending with you on all fours and my cock deep inside your cunt."

Willow shivers, lips curling into a grin. "Okay."

Before I can get another taste, Willow turns and with her back against my chest, she shoots. No doubt or pause, and immediately, Glen falls to the side. His chest heaves. The bullet has done its damage, and a wheezing sound emits from his mouth while the puddle around him grows.

They scream. Curses and pleas for help.

The sound is loud and full of anguish while Willow unloads another shot, this time to his side. At the impact, Glen bounces on the sand, and the wheezing becomes gargles.

"You bitch," Stella cries out, attempting to stand up but wobbles on her injured leg. Two steps toward my wife; that's all she gets before crumbling, gripping the sand while trying to crawl closer. Another discharge. More blood. "Stop! Please!"

"How much do you care for him if you were willing to sleep with what's mine?" *Christ,* her possessiveness is sexy. "Answer me before the next one is to his head."

Stella grits her teeth, refusing to answer, something Willow doesn't like. My girl's ruthless like this, and I'm turned on by it. *I'm going to fuck you so good, bunny. Give you what you need.*

"Still want to play the silent game? Fine." Willow smirks, and before Stella can take in another breath, my bunny pulls the trigger. This time her mark is Glen's head.

That ends him, and they lose it. Both women move toward the body but are stopped by the guards, and the cries that rend the air are painful. Irritating to my ear.

"Silence."

Willow turns her head and looks up at me from beneath long lashes. "Did you have plans for him, because I found the man useless?"

"You handled it beautifully, my love." Lowering my head, I nip her jaw. "Besides, now there are no distractions for them. Do you have any questions?"

"I do." In her eyes, I see my future and it's the same for her. Willow's expression when on me is soft and sweet, full of love. "One that's been bugging me since I realized you weren't the person in those pictures."

I know what she's talking about. I've seen the photographs and it's taken everything in me not to snap Stella and Calliope's necks, but I managed and it's all because of the woman who owns my heart. This is her moment. She's owed this.

"Go on," I say with a quick tap to her ass. "Ask them."

"Thank you." My girl's attention lingers on my face for a few more seconds before she turns and walks toward the two. These are answers she needs, and I will not deny her. Once close, she drops with her butt sitting on her heels. "Look at me, Stella." Her voice is soft, and in her grief, the other woman complies. Almost trance-like. "The pictures were with Glen, weren't they?"

"Fuck you."

"I'm trying to be merciful."

While my bunny handles her nemesis, I turn to my family. For a little while, I take them in as the scene unfolds behind me. I listen while my wife gets her answers, and through it all, they've been watching with smiles of approval and pride on their faces.

"How do you vote?"

"Would it change if I disagreed?" my father asks and I shake my head, matching his smirk. "Good."

"Then?"

"Death." No hesitation. No remorse.

"And you two?"

Everly and Adam also nod in agreement, but before either can say a single word, we hear it. A body thumps to the ground, and our heads whip toward the shore.

Motherfuck, bunny.

I feel the bead of pre-come as it beads at the tip of my cock and rolls down the shaft before caressing my balls. Willow is atop Stella while Joe holds a gun to Calliope's head, forcing her to stand on shaky legs and watch as my wife beats her daughter.

The Glock in Willow's hand comes down across the blonde's face, much like I did to Glen with the brass knuckles, and her nose breaks. There's blood on her hands, a few drops on her cheeks, and the beautiful dress on her body is ruined. She's brutal with each blow, but it's her words that I focus on.

"You forced me away from the man that I love with those pictures, you sick bitch. You tore me from my family and friends— time I'll never get back—and all for what?" It's rhetorical, yet she needs to get this off her chest. "For greed? Personal amusement?"

"Stop her, Flavio!" Calliope thrashes in Joe's hold, yet he doesn't move an inch. "Please...I-I'm begging you. S-save us!"

We ignore her idiocy and watch Willow unleash another sharp strike, this time to Stella's temple and the woman's eyes roll back. Not that my wife allows her to pass out. She lifts the blonde's head off the wet sand by her hair, yanking until a chunk falls out and she cries.

"No more," Stella says, voice hoarse. Coughing.

"You and your mother ruined my life." Willow lowers her face down to hers, lips almost touching. "I'm only returning the favor."

14

Willow

A Few Minutes Prior…

"*I* fucked Glen in Silas's bed."

While her words are low, to me it's as if she's screamed them from the tallest building. The words are cohesive—truthful—and if there was a small shred of empathy left in my body, it died at that moment. So many emotions and memories rush at me that it's hard to keep up, but the prevalent one is the smirk on her face when she threw those photos at me.

Gleeful.

Egotistical.

Maniacal.

Funny thing is, I'm the one on the other side of the coin this time and for a second, I close my eyes. The thread of sanity I'm fighting to hold on to is slipping, stretching more and more, and then she laughs, digging into those frayed edges.

Her chuckle is low and holds a bit of condescension while the tears continue to fall. A contradiction of emotions, but the hostility inside her wins out. Moreover, I don't regret killing him.

He's nothing to me in the grand scheme of things.

"You wore that same idiotic look back then, too. As if your heart had been ripped out, and fuck, do I love it."

Before she's finished, my eyes snap open and focus on her, my finger moving toward the trigger. "I'm not the same woman, Stella. Life has taught me cruelty, and I plan to pay it forward."

"I've enjoyed your pain over the years, Willow," she says, ignoring the threat in my words. Because I'm not the same girl who landed in Curacao just yesterday, and it's all thanks to Silas. He's opened my eyes. Accepts me as is—encourages the slight madness that everyone tries to hide. I hadn't allowed myself to feel anything past self-pity and loathing for years, but now that the chains have broken, I feel free.

I'm angry and a little bitter over the time lost.

I'm full of relief and happiness and more importantly, love.

It's why I would—and will—kill these women before the night is through. *No one will ever come between us again.*

Moreover, I'm at peace with this decision. No regret or remorse.

"I set up the camera and took the pictures of Glen using my body to gift you." Stella brings a hand to her face and furiously wipes the tears falling, her lips trembling. Pain radiates from her every pore, and the way she chokes on a sob each time her stare wavers to her fallen lover shouldn't make me happy, but it does. *So morbid.* "We fucked throughout his home. The bed being our favorite."

"What else did you do?"

"I hate you."

"The feeling's mutual." Turning toward Calliope and Joe, I narrow my eyes. "Force her to her knees."

"As you wish." At once, he bumps the back of her legs and she drops, harshly thumping on the wet sand.

Without looking at anyone, I walk over to Calliope and grip her hair, forcing her head back. There's a yelp and a curse, the sound of Stella trying to rush in our direction, but that injured leg stops her. Instead, she watches me through watery eyes and with a horror-filled expression while I place the muzzle of the dirty—blood-stained—gun into her mother's mouth.

"I won't ask you again." My tone is harsh, and the words are enunciated through clenched teeth. "What. Did. You. Do?"

"Stop." So weak. Now she's pathetic.

"Five...four...three—"

"We paid an addict to dye her hair blonde and crash into you after consuming her earnings in coke."

"Anything else?" Her mother gags when I push the metal tip in deeper.

"We should've put the explosive in your car and not the one who crashed into you." Even through her pain and tears, the woman has a challenging bite to her tone. *So stupid.* "My Glen would be alive if I did."

And because they've decimated any empathy I could have for them with their cruelty, I laugh. "But you didn't."

Calliope gags again, her saliva dribbling down her chin. She looks dirty and a bit broken; nothing like the conceited woman that lied and put her hands on me before I left.

"Why are you here?" I ask, realizing my mistake in opening the door without looking through the peephole. "You said all you needed to, two days ago."

"I'm here because I care, Willow." Her expression is soft, and I'm thrown off. Just like I've been since— "Please. Let's sit and talk."

"No. Thank you." The façade drops then and she pushes

forward, knocking my still-healing body into the doorframe. And still, even as my body freezes in pain, I halt her with an arm across the chest. Calliope isn't the tallest woman and is slight in build; it doesn't take much to halt her steps. "Leave."

"Of course, but first..." She digs into her handbag and pulls out her cell phone. Without taking her eyes off mine, she presses a single number and then the speaker option. It rings three times; each one seems to have an eternity between them, and then he answers. Immediately, my heart flutters and my lungs seize.

"What do you want?" Silas answers, voice terse.

"Silas, darling. I'm at the place now." Calliope smiles at me. "They're being difficult."

"Can they hear me?"

"Yes, son."

There's an annoyed grunt at her calling him that, but then I pay attention to his words. "...then I never want to see or hear from her again. Understood?" I'm nodding, but no words come out. My throat feels closed off. "Verbal response."

"Loud and clear," his stepmother answers for me. I couldn't even if I wanted to.

"You have forty-eight hours. Use them wisely, and don't bother me again."

The call drops as soon as the last syllable passes through his lips, and I'm left aching for a different reason: he doesn't want to see me. This hurts more than the accident and pictures combined.

"You heard him, Willow. Forty-eight hours." Faster than I realize, there's a burning pain in my ribs and her elbow digs deeper. "Next, it'll be cops here to arrest you."

They?

They?

Who the hell was the *they* she was referring to? Why did it take me so long to realize she never once said my name?

"Who were you talking about that day?" I ask the woman

kneeling with a mouth full of gun, but before she can reply, another voice pulls my attention. Then, it just doesn't matter.

"All I needed to do was marry Silas. Simple enough and would've solved everything." Every instinct in me rebels at the mere thought that without me in the picture it could've happened, but I bite back the rage and let her talk. Stella isn't talking to me, though. Her stare is on Glen, and a shuddering breath rocks her.

"Please stop!" It's muffled by the Glock, but I ignore Calliope. "Someone, help me!"

Not both of them. Just her.

Selfish bitch.

But I spare her for the moment; just until I finish with Stella. With a quick strike, one punch to her mouth, she slumps over with a menacing Joe already reaching for her. He understands what I want without me uttering a single word, gripping her by the arm before forcing her to kneel again.

Stella's mine, but *she* will be for the family.

It's only fair.

Maybe I should feel some guilt—this is Flavio's wife after all—but there's nothing in me.

Nothing but the need for answers. To end this and move on.

"Your hatred of me has never made sense. Why did Silas matter, if you loved Glen?" I ask while patting the older woman on the cheek condescendingly. "Or were you using him too?"

"I loved him!"

"Then why?"

"Simple." For a second she turns her face toward Calliope, and I'm surprised by the quick flash of regret in her expression. Both make a pitiful sight at the moment, but it disappears just as fast as it appeared. "People like you don't deserve a man like Silas, and you didn't stay in your lane, Willow. Rich men need a woman like me; the right pedigree and education—"

"This coming from the woman born from a cheating father and whore mother?"

"Did he ever tell you about the time he fucked my mouth a year after—" She doesn't get to finish as I tackle her to the ground, straddling her chest and land the first blow. Then another. The Glock in my hand breaks her nose with a single hit. And I'm a bloody mess for it.

From my skin to dress, I'm filthy without repentance.

It's as if I'm in a tunnel and *he fucked my mouth* reverberates all around me.

"You forced me away from the man that I love with those pictures, you sick bitch. You tore me from my family and friends— time I'll never get back, and for what?" Moans of pain come from her mouth and her hands weakly try to push me away, but I'm too consumed by my ire. "For greed? Personal amusement?"

"Stop her, Flavio!" Calliope says, but for some reason, it's coming out low. Almost a whisper. "Please...I-I'm begging you. S-save us!"

My reply to her pleas is another direct hit to her daughter's temple, and I smile when her eyes roll back. But not. She doesn't get off that easily; I lift Stella's head off the wet sand by her hair, yanking until a chunk falls out and she whimpers.

Begs me.

"No more," Stella coughs. Her voice full of so much pain.

"You and your mother ruined my life." I lower my face down to hers until they hover. Just a hair's breadth between us. "Now, I'm only returning the favor. Your ego has always been your downfall, and watching you suffer through Glen's death has brought me peace. It's why I killed him first; I knew your heart would break."

The sound is loud in the dead of night, its consequence taking mere seconds from entering Stella's head and exiting out the back. Pulling the trigger was almost an out-of-body experience, and I exhale slowly as she drops back with a hole just above the bridge of her nose that quickly fills with overflowing blood. Her death is fast, not nearly enough, but the right punishment for the crime.

Never come between a woman and her man.

15
SILAS

"*W*illow."

That snaps her attention toward me, and her eyes widen when they meet. There's a hint of fear in them, worry, but it's irrational. My smile tells her as much, and I don't take it personally because ending a life is never easy, and my beautiful bunny took care of two.

Just like there's an up, this crash will come, and I'll spoil her through it.

Later. Much later.

Right now, I need her.

Slowly, she stands and walks over without looking at either body.

To be honest, I don't even think she hears the wails from Calliope or notices the way she tried to lunge at her. Not that she made it a single step before my father walked over and whispered something in her ear.

Whatever he said, it took the fight clear from her, and now she's limp in Joe's hold.

"Hi," she says, voice low and so sweet while the gun slips from her fingers. It thumps on the ground, a muted sound she's unaware of. "I might've lost my cool there."

"I saw."

"Are you mad?"

A grin tugs at my lips, cock so hard it hurts. "Not at all."

"Good." A sigh leaves her, the sound full of relief, but then Willow's brows furrow. Her head tilts from side to side, searching for our missing family. "Oh, God." Hands shaking, she takes a step back and I don't like it. Not one bit. "Are they calling the police on me?"

"Come here."

"Silas, I—"

In one stride I have her in my arms and my lips on hers, the kiss rough. It takes her by surprise and she gasps, giving me the opportunity to slip my tongue into her mouth. She's sweet and pliant in my arms, melting against me while I explore and take and fucking show her through my touch that she's mine.

Always.

There is no end. No separation.

I'd kill my own family if they ever rose against her.

Once I know she's calm, I slow my kiss to gentle bites and soft pecks, dragging my teeth down her abused lips before pulling back to stare into warm eyes. They're glossy, a bit hooded, and her desire causes a deep rumble to grow in my chest.

At this moment, with blood on the ground and specks over her flesh, I've never found her more beautiful.

Today, she killed for me.

Because she saw a threat and eliminated what tried to come between us.

"Everyone's headed to the airport, love." Another kiss. Just because the expression on her face is near drunk, as if I'm her drug. "Adam and Everly are starting their two-week honeymoon in Greece while my father has plans of his own. The guards also have their orders to vacate the premise, but stay in Curacao."

"Plans?" she asks with a raised brow. "Just like that?"

"Yes, beautiful. Just like that." Turning her in my arms, I make her face the bodies and a sobbing Calliope. And I'm proud of her for not tensing. "He's heading to the Bahamas for some golfing with a few buddies of his."

"So he's not mad?"

"At you? Never."

"Thank you."

"Baby girl, when I said this was our family apology to you, I meant it. These three were yours to do with as you pleased. You held their lives in your hands, and had you not acted, I would've slit their throats while you slept."

"You're serious?"

"I am." My lips skim down her temple and cheek until I reach the area just below her ear and nip. The sharp bite pulls a hiss from her, but I soften the sting with the tip of my tongue. "They've caused enough damage. Don't you think?"

Calliope watches us through bloodshot eyes, her makeup ruined and body filthy. She's gone silent now, not that it matters either way, and I know it's because she knows she's next. No exit. No one to save her.

"Yes."

"Good girl." Nuzzling her fragrant skin, I give a short hum and pull back. "She's the perfect example of unchecked gluttony." Because there's a difference between ambition and greed. "It was never enough to be my father's wife; she wanted it all. The business, money—the connections and power." My hand travels up Willow's arm and to her neck, to the necklace she never takes off. I finger the chain and then the pendant, watching the full moon glinting off the precious stone. "Calliope never cared for us, but more what we could do for her status-wise. The plan at first was for Stella to charm me, gain access to my bed, and then claim she was pregnant. But then you came into the picture. You were an immediate threat, sweetheart, because I could no longer be manipulated."

"They're all sick."

"Agreed." Dropping the pendant, I wrap my hand around her throat and turn her face toward me. Our eyes meet, and I smile before nuzzling her nose. "Originally, she was going to push for me to marry Stella as the right thing to do. They'd fake a pregnancy, force my hand, and kill me a few months later so she could be with Glen. Of course, with me out of the picture, he'd step in as my father's successor since Everly wants no part in King Aviation; they'd have complete control through him, although his plans were vastly different from theirs."

"You ruined everything." Calliope stares at Willow in my arms, eyes full of rage. Not that my girl pays her any mind. Instead, my bunny bites my chin. "I should've killed—"

"Enough," I growl, and Charlotte steps closer to them. She slaps a hand over my stepmother's mouth. "Take her away. We'll deal with her later."

"Yes, sir." The guards turn, each gripping one of Calliope's arms, but my girl stops them with a hand up. That causes me to raise a brow; she's a boss and has no idea.

"What's going to happen to her?"

"I'll deal with her, love. She'll get the ending she deserves."

"I trust you, but..."

"But?"

"What if she doesn't die yet."

"Go on." I almost snort at the relief on my stepmother's face. Instead, I look down and give Willow my full attention. "You have my full support, baby."

"Okay." Taking in a deep breath, she exhales slowly while gathering her thoughts. Not that it takes long. Willow nods to herself, and I fall in love with the devious glint in her gaze. How she loses the self-doubt and straightens her back; I see the effect of my words taking place. "What if she goes to jail for a little while instead? What if we take away all the jewelry and money and social status? She should pay for the death of her children and the unknown woman who crashed into me. Nothing will hurt her more than losing it all, experiencing the full brunt of failure, before her end."

"Done." My eyes only leave hers long enough to give the guards direction. "Call the prime minister and have it taken care of. She can serve her time here." That's when the thrashing and cursing begins; Calliope fights them until Joe throws her over his shoulder and turns to walk away. They make it a few feet before I call her name, and Charlotte forces her head up by the hair. "Your biggest mistake was going after what's mine, *dear.* Every tear she's shed—every night away from me—is going to cost you. You'll beg me for death soon enough."

With that they take her, and I take a step away from my wife.

Then another.

I stop between the dead bodies and take in the damage she caused. *Fuck, my little killer is magnificent.* Each bullet discharged hit its mark. The wounds are precise and neat.

But now, it's time for me to play. I've been nice and patient and indulgent.

"Run, Willow."

That caught her off guard, and her brows furrow. "What?"

"Run, baby." Stepping out of my shoes, I remove my socks and then my pants. Not wearing anything underneath; I'm hard and fist myself—stroke my dick to the rise and fall of her chest while she never takes her eyes off me. They shift between my face and length, but she takes heed and moves back a few paces. "A real man knows when to stand back and let his woman shine. And you did tonight, beautiful. *Fuck*, you were glorious in your thirst for revenge, but right now it's my turn to hunt."

"Silas, I'm not sure—"

"You have ten seconds." I close my eyes and my chest expands as I take in a deep breath. Between my need, one I've been controlling since the first time she fired the gun, and the gratifying indulgence of violence, I'm past waiting. Don't want to.

The soft footfalls catch my attention next, and I begin to count from ten to one in a slow progression while a cool breeze skims across my heated flesh. I relax my stance and then open my eyes.

I find her at once.

Running. Heading down the beach, and I don't hesitate to give chase.

My pace is faster than hers, determined, and her squeal when she looks back is a thunderbolt to my cock. Beads of pre-come slip from the head and onto the sand, leaving a trail of my desire while dead bodies linger at the shore. She's fast, I'll give her that, but within seconds my arm is around her waist and I'm lifting her up while my bunny gasps.

The sound is almost as decadent as her moans.

With her back to my bare chest, I bring her against me and lower my mouth to her ear. Just hover there, taking her sweet scent into my lungs while goose bumps rise across her skin. For a few minutes we stay like this, just being after so long, but then I feel her move against me.

It's subtle at first, a small shift of her fabric-covered ass over my length, but then she gets bolder. Her thighs squeeze together. Her hand reaches back, trying to pull me closer, and my patience snaps.

The flimsy fabric of her dress lies in tatters on the ground beneath us a second later, leaving my beautiful wife naked and with nothing separating us.

"Silas," she keens, arching against me when my hands cup her breasts, jiggling them a bit in my palms before slapping each tip twice. They bead tightly, so pretty and sweet. "This is insane. I shouldn't want to—"

"But you do." Pinching her nipples, I pull the sensitive tips and enjoy the sight of her fighting instinct. To pull away. To offer more. "You're my other half, Willow. The better part of my soul, and we deserve happiness."

"We do."

"I've missed you, bunny." My touch is rougher, squeezing her tits before tracing down her abdomen with one hand and up to her neck with the other. She's pliant in my arms, shivering in anticipation, and this time there will be no pause. "Missed your smile. Your scent. The way your cunt always drips for me."

"Oh, God."

"Not God, bunny. *I'm* your owner." I tighten my hold on her pussy, cupping her while adding pressure to her swollen labia and clit. She's throbbing, trying to gyrate against my palm—I give her bundle of nerves a sharp flick with the tips of two fingers.

Immediately, she cries out and her thighs shake. I'm not surprised by her quick orgasm; she's always been sensitive and free with me.

A rush of warm heat soaks my hand and wrist, causing a shiver to rush down my spine. I feel her release as if it were my own, but I need more. All of her.

Before she's done shaking, I have her on all fours for me with her knees spread. The sand is wet, and water laps a few feet from us—a tinge of frothy red skimming along the shoreline as the DNA of the two bodies mix with the dark waters.

Later tonight or early in the morning, this place will be full of police pretending to investigate. They'll rope off the area, although unnecessary since it's private land, and go through the motions for the news media that's surely to come for the story.

After all, a prominent businessman's wife committed a heinous act.

My cock slips through her lips, spreading her wetness from her entrance to clit, and then taps her asshole once. I've had her there, worshipped her, but now I'm owed another payment.

One forceful thrust and I'm inside of her tight, wet heat. Immediately her walls grip. They clench and flutter while my girl moans, body shuddering beneath me. *Motherfucking heaven.*

"I love you," I grit out, thrusting through each quake of her body. Willow's wetness coats me from cock to balls—the squelching noises mingle with the sound coming from the surf, and it's a melody that soothes me. It calms that animalistic urge to chain her to me and not let her out of my sight. "Never again, bunny. You're never leaving me."

"I love you, Silas. I'm here." A vow. Promise. And I reward her with a harder slam of my hips, taking what's mine with wild abandon. Her asscheeks bounce, the round flesh rippling with each piston while my fingers at her hips dig in deeper, more than likely leaving small print-sized bruises behind. She doesn't complain, though. Instead, my wife turns her head and meets my eyes with hooded ones of her own. "And I'm sorry."

Three words, and they destroy what's left of my anger.

It's been simmering since she left, this small sense of betrayal. My mind understood the circumstances, her fear and flight response, but there's always been this small disappointment that she didn't come to me for help.

I know Calliope changed my gate code.

I know they threatened her with my anger and jail time.

I know my broken phone during my trip didn't help.

"You should've fought for me. For us," I grit out through clenched teeth, holding her in place while I take what's mine. My wife. My life. "Know that I have you, love. I'd never abandon you no matter what you do or what happens."

"Believe you," she hisses on the next hard thrust, her fingers digging into the sand, but she doesn't find purchase. "You're everything to me."

"Fuck. *Fuck.*" Pleasure seeps through me at that, settling on my heavy balls and then the tip of my cock. It's near painful, yet I clench my jaw and bury myself to the hilt, emptying every last drop inside her warm pussy. Spurt after spurt fills her, her walls pulsing around me pulling me in deeper, and I lift a hand and spank her.

Just once. Hard.

The solid blow stings my hand but sets her off, and my beautiful wife turns the pain into bliss. She comes again, nearly falling flat onto the sand, but I hold her right where she is—on all fours and whimpering, unable to hold still as wave after wave takes her under.

And I love the feel and milking of her walls. How incoherent and sensitive she becomes—how those little panting breaths she releases make me feel like a fucking king.

The silence that ensues isn't uncomfortable. Instead, it lets us reconnect in a different way, and while I know she thought coming here was a mistake, I proved her wrong. I'm her home as she is mine. She's my other half, and I'm her lobster.

In this life and the next.

"I need a shower," she whispers after a while, a small huff following. "I'm filthy."

"Like you like this." Slowly, I pull out and move back just enough to see some of my come drip out of her. "Dirty and full of me."

"You would." There's a small snort, then a hiss when she shifts and I'm quick to my feet, scooping her into my arms. We're not far from the back of our home and I head there, making sure to keep my hold tight on her. Her face is in my neck, her warm puffs of breath caressing my skin. "But that leads me to a very important and serious question, Silas."

"Which is?" Turning my head, I lay a tiny kiss on her forehead. Breathe in deep and let her sweet scent fill my lungs. "Ask me and it's yours."

"How much time do I get to plan our wedding?"

I stop at that, giving my shoulder a small jerk. "Look at me."

"No. I'm comfortable and tired."

That pulls a laugh from me. One that's loud and shakes us. "Please." Warm, sated eyes peek up at me from beneath long lashes, and my heart thumps harshly inside my chest. This feels right. No more anger or lies or threats. Just us. As it should always have been. "Today, tomorrow—six months from now. It doesn't matter, as long as you're happy and always by my side."

"I love you, Silas."

"And you are my world, bunny."

EPILOGUE

Silas

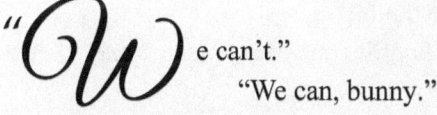

Six Months Later…
Wedding Day

"We can't."

"We can, bunny."

"But, Silas," she whines in that keening little tone that causes my cock to throb. More so as I take her in this simple white dress, her growing belly showing for the world to see. Pregnancy looks so good on my Willow—my little slut is always aroused—and today I'm blessed to finally give her the wedding stolen from us by circumstance.

The Grecian-style gown teases my senses with its tight bust, emphasizing her perfect tits, that then flows over her bump before showing off just enough leg to make my mouth water. And I'm salivating for her, enjoying the feel of heat beneath my fingertips while I kiss the back of her neck.

My wife is nothing short of perfection. But then again, she's a goddess.

Born to be mine.

Lifting the back of her dress, I grip her right asscheek in one hand and squeeze. "Spread your legs, baby. I want to say *I do* with your juices drying on my cock."

"Oh fuck," she moans, but does as I ask, helping me hold her dress out of the way while bending over just a bit. Our home in Curacao is where my beautiful girl wanted to get married, right near the edge of the water where we made a family pact in blood. With the low evening sky growing dimmer and the guests already drinking, we planned the intimate affair with who we are in mind.

No more hiding.

It's in our DNA, as my cousin Malcolm would say. *Because spilling blood to protect your family is an honor.* And that bastard has no place in his heart for anyone but his wife; he revolves around London.

As it should be.

Your family is important, you are responsible for them, but I'd die for Willow without thinking twice. She owns me as I own her, and of that, there's never been a doubt.

And the Asher and King families are very much alike in that sense.

"Always so wet for me," I groan out, clenching my teeth when her tiny hole flutters against the head of my cock. Almost kissing the tip. "I love you."

"Love you," she moans out, reaching back with her free hand to grab my hair. The deeper I slide in, the harder she tugs, and I enjoy the sting. How tight she grips, then flutters—her hips pushing back

—to pull me in deeper. "God, I love the feeling of you in me. Stretching me."

"Motherfuck." Those words send electrical pulses through me. Her need for me makes me feel a hundred feet tall, and when I pull out and she cries out, I'm the king of the world. "You're my heaven, Willow. Today, tomorrow, and always."

"Please, Silas. Need you."

"Behave." I stop when just the tip is inside, gripping her hip tight with one hand while the other slips up her neck and to her lips, smearing the lip gloss before dipping inside her warm mouth. "Be a good girl and wet them for me."

Those hooded eyes darken. "Yes, Daddy."

My eyes close for a second; Willow knows what those words do to me.

Moreover, she's been doing it since we found out during a trip to Ireland that we're expecting.

Such a good daddy.

Daddy, feed me.

My pussy needs her daddy.

"Suck, bunny. Show me how filthy you are." At my command, her tongue swirls around the digits, coating them in her spit. The vanity mirror provides a private show to every reaction, the loving way she pulls them in deeper until gagging before opening her mouth so I can see them glistening on her tongue. "My perfect girl."

"Please, Silas." The walls of her cunt contract, her entrance squeezing the head of my cock, and I reward her impatience with a smack to her clit. Her spit and juices spread over her, the sound making me smile while she arches against my hold.

Yet I don't fuck her. Not yet.

Another smack, and she lifts onto the tip of her toes. Her cries are loud inside the room. *My perfection.*

But it's when I pinch her throbbing bundle of nerves, orgasm slamming into her, that I sink in deep and chase my own release.

Because my girl always comes first; on my mouth, by my fingers, or by my cock.

"Oh, God! Silas, I—" My next thrust causes her eyes to roll back and skin to flush, juices running down her thighs and onto the floor below. Tiny wet noises fill the room along with her moans and my grunts.

I'm unable to talk.

She feels too good. So wet and tight and *beautiful.*

So I show her through each thrust how crazed I am for her. I fuck her through each shiver—each pulse of pleasure she's drowning in—and take her flesh as the gift it is.

This is our wedding. We're one.

One heart. One soul. One breath.

"You're all I'll ever need, Willow. Till death and beyond. Just you." Another rush of pleasure grips her, and those fingers in my hair tighten to the point of pain, anchoring herself to me as I rub her clit a little harder. This orgasm overtakes her and she whimpers—body flushed—as I slam in and out.

I'm riding her hard. Strokes near punishing.

"Daddy, I love you."

"Son of a bitch," I grit out, thrusting deep while pressing my chest to her back. My cock pulses, rope after rope of come filling her cunt while my beautiful wife's words are on repeat. *Daddy.* Willow has no idea how easily she controls me with that.

For a while we stay like that; joined and close, but I know she gets tired easily nowadays. Twins will do that to you, a boy and a girl, and I pull out.

There's a loveseat not far from us and I walk us over, placing her in my lap while she catches her breath. Her hair is a little bit of a mess and I push a stray curl away from her face, my finger lingering on her cheek while sweet brown eyes shine at me with so much love.

"You okay, bunny?"

"Mhhm."

"Need a nap?"

"Uh-uh."

"Can I get some words out of you?" I say while my hand slips between her legs. My release has dripped all over her thighs, but I catch the bit just outside her entrance and push it back inside. *Where it belongs.*

"I need a nap and my dress is ruined, Silas." There's a smile in that reproach that I find adorable. "Told you we shouldn't."

"How about you close those pretty eyes, I tell everyone to eat first, and then you get dressed in the replica I had made of this lovely little number."

"You had this planned." Not a question. An accusation with a hint of amusement.

"More like I was a boy scout in a past life and came prepared for the inevitable."

Willow huffs, but I catch the quirk of her lips. "I should be mad."

"But you're not."

"No." She shakes her sleepy head. "I'm not."

"Good girl." Laying a protective hand over our baby bump, I stroke the skin there softly while she relaxes. It takes a few minutes for her low snores to greet my ears and it's the sweetest sound, reminds me of how lucky I am that her path in life crossed mine.

I'm thankful to the deities above.

I'm in debt to life for our unborn children.

And I'll take care of them both. Give my life and take one as well if it means they're safe and happy.

"LATE TO YOUR OWN WEDDING? Seems like a common occurrence with the men I associate with," a voice says as I enter the kitchen after leaving my bunny to sleep. She's tucked in and warm while I deal with the rest, but the person in the room stops me in my tracks. My cousin stands not too far from me, drink in hand and clear amusement on his face. "Good to see you, Silas."

"This coming from you is rich, cousin. Although Mariah's worse than you." Walking over, I take his offered hand, but the fucker pulls me into a quick hug. He's never been the most affectionate, and I'm caught off guard for a second but then squeeze him just as tight. We spent a lot of time together as kids and got into just as much trouble. "Thank you for coming to the wedding. We appreciate it."

"Wouldn't miss it for the world." He's pensive for a minute—slow—while taking another sip from his glass, but I see through the calm façade. It's something both sides of the family have; we're ruthless in business and out. We also never pass up the opportunity to make a good deal. "How busy is your schedule for the rest of the year? Say October through December?

"Very, but adjustments can be made for the right reason." There's a poured drink beside him, a few fingers' worth of his favorite spirit, and I tilt my head toward it. Malcolm passes the glass without pause. "Why? What do you need?"

"I have a proposition for you, Silas." He smirks and then raises his gin in a silent toast. "A very lucrative one."

Clinking my tumbler with his, I nod. "You have my attention."

"Good. Because I need a pilot and an untraceable private plane."

OUTTAKE

Silas

The Day She Met Her Future…

"Are you sure this is the man on your surveillance footage?" I ask Thiago—the next in line for the De Leon syndicate in Miami—while tapping my fingers atop the table. He couldn't be here in person due to an earlier meeting, but he's watching the interrogation through a set-up screen.

His expression is murderous, his presence felt, and it makes the man currently strapped to a chair across from me whimper.

It's a lovely sound, and I smile.

He's in pain and writhing, eyes shifting around the room in search of help, but he'll find no one. Not a soul will come near this unit, and even if they did, those who have permission will ignore it without remorse.

We're inside a strip mall not far from the university and a stretch of businesses that cater to its students. It's a busy location, over-crowded and at times rowdy, but easy to come and go undetected as I mix in with the crowd. They know me, I'm one of them, but fear is a precarious thing.

For as curious as they are, most stay away.

They heed the warnings. The darkness that surrounds me.

I'm not here to make friends or build life-lasting relationships. And all it took was one simple act of violence against a drunken frat boy deciding to use me as a pledging tool a year ago. He wanted to impress, to look good in front of his brothers, but I'm not the one.

The rule is simple: fuck around and fight out.

A single blow to his temple made him stumble. A second had him on his back, eyes dazed while I mounted his torso. Every single bloody punch, elbow, and kick after was a wordless message: stay clear.

If you see me? Look away.

You hear me talking? Run.

Moreover, no one questions my disappearances or follows me.

"I-It's a mistake. I-I'd never—"

Ignoring my guest, I keep my attention on the screen. Thiago nods, his jaw ticking and the palpable ire causes the other man to sweat profusely. "I am."

"And what did he take?"

"Fifteen bricks and half the cash logged onto the flight."

"I see." Turning toward my ex-employee, I narrow my eyes. This man is a loader. Nothing else. He's been with the company for less than three months and knows the consequences, yet, he still chose to tempt fate. *Fucking idiot.*

"Please, Mr. King...I—" He's silenced by a hand over his mouth, the guard placing the muzzle of his Glock against the now pallid asshole. The act causes him to shake, tears rolling down his grimy cheeks, but I'm not moved. If anything, I find his fear repulsively annoying.

Life is simple, yet so many are hellbent on creating difficulties for themselves.

Know your place.

Don't touch what isn't yours.

Moreover, Pierce Lewis forgot those simple commands. Instructions are given both verbally and in writing to every new hire during their orientation. This is also reiterated in the NDA on file carrying their signatures so those working for us don't find themselves in these situations.

King's Aviation doesn't allow mistakes. He knew this. The stench of guilt surrounds him.

The moronic behavior astounds me. How can someone be so stupid?

"Release him, Joe."

"As you wish, sir." The action is rough, the shove Pierce receives almost tips the chair forward, and I chuckle. Even De Leon laughs. This guard and his wife have been with my family for years, always faithful, and will have a new task as of tomorrow morning. "My apologies."

"None needed." Standing from my seat, I crane my neck from side to side, stretching the muscles there before rolling up my sleeves. Normally, I'd just remove my shirt, but today the ruined garment will come in handy.

Another pitiful cry from Pierce and it reverberates throughout the room. The sound echoes, bouncing off unfinished walls, while in the distance the deep rumble of a forklift drowns it out. Heavy machinery kicks on next in another form, a little closer this time, and you can almost make out the whisper of voices talking not far from where he's pissed himself.

People. His only salvation.

"Help!" A scream. A desperate plea. "Please, someone help me!"

Nothing. Not so much as a pause from those outside these walls.

This plot of land and the building I'm currently working out of are all owned by my family under a shell corporation. There are no legal ties to King Aviation, but we need the quiet and *under-construction* location for certain business practices.

Even those working on-site are paid generously to ignore the sounds coming from this empty office space. The would-be-in-the-future dentist's office is large and a bit dusty, but the back accommodates my needs just fine. There's plenty of room to interrogate someone and carry out sentencing if need be.

In the future, though, it'll become a community plaza with leased units for various businesses, but that won't be until after *she* graduates. This place makes it easy for me to keep track of the shy little beauty I plan to make mine. I watch her at all hours.

Always close. I'm her personal bodyguard.

"Are you done?" I ask Pierce, brow raised.

"Please." Low now. Pathetic. It's dawning on him how truly fucked he is.

"Answer the question, Mr. Lewis."

"I don't want to die."

"And I have somewhere to be, yet I'm here dealing with you." Atop the small table, there are two weapons: a knife and a gun. Each one is silver, the metal glinting in the room's low lighting, and there are specs of dried blood on the sharp edge. "We don't always get what we want."

"I'll leave. Disappear."

"You will."

One thing this idiot didn't do was act alone. He was enticed by another employee, and after giving my guard a nod, he turns on another large screen. On it, the lifeless body of his accomplice lies unmoving and surrounded by a large pool of blood. A middle-aged man with a huge gambling debt and poor judgment.

One instigated. The other acted.

"Oh, God," he cries out in earnest now, thrashing and shaking so violently he makes himself sick. The putrid stench overflows, rushing down his chest and legs, staining my table, too. "No. No. NO!"

"Where's the money, Pierce? Where's my customer's merchandise?"

His mouth is open, but no words come out. Instead, his focus is on the blade. The same one I used on his associate; I cut off each finger of his right hand and made him swallow them before slitting his throat.

"Five. Four. Three—"

"At the motel room, he rents on a week-to-week basis."

"Where in the room?" I ask, my pointer finger tapping the sharp-tipped weapon.

"A/C vent to the left of his bed."

"Good boy." Flicking my gaze toward Thiago, I nod in confirmation. "Are your men there?"

"Yes. Ivan will pick up and drop off."

"Joe will be here and personally escort it overseas."

"Thank you, my friend."

I'm shaking my head before Thiago finished. "My apologies for the inconvenience. This won't happen again."

"I know." His chuckle is deep, loud, and then cut off by the knocking on a door. At once, his face relaxes and I know it's Luna. A man only reacts that way when his woman is involved and I understand him. I'm overtaken by the same demonic need I recognize in his eyes. "My family trusts yours, Silas. The Asher and King businesses never disappoint."

"Your confidence is appreciated." Another shy knock and he drums his fingers in impatience. Wanting to answer. My response to that is a swift decision; I grab the gun and empty the clip before anyone can question me. Each bullet enters his skull, disfiguring his face while the impact causes Pierce to bounce in his seat.

Blood stains my clothes.

Remnants of his brain splatter across every surface.

He's dead and there's somewhere important I need to be.

As does Thiago who ends the connection with a smile.

"I'll take care of everything, Mr. King. It's almost time."

"Thank you, Joe. Keep in contact." With that I leave, heading straight for the back door. There's a hose here and I'm quick to rinse off, shedding off my long sleeve shirt and tossing it just inside the door. The clean-up crew knows to pick up back here and so does my guard; he's meticulous.

As is his wife. Moreover, it's the reason they'll be assigned to my bunny.

The dark pants will stay on, for now, they're clean except for the bottom right, and I'm in a hurry. Not that she notices a few minutes later when I bump into her outside the lecture hall, making sure her body falls against me.

"Oh shit!" she teeters and yelps, clutching my arms to stay upright and I'm more than willing to oblige, while her books fall to the ground. My right hand grips her hip, squeezing a bit to hold her in place while this electric current flows between her body and mine. It stings. Burns me, and by the bright look in those sweet chocolate orbs, she feels it too.

"You okay, sweetheart?"

"Yes." A bit breathy. Nervous yet intrigued. "Are you?"

"I am now." There's no questioning look at my response, instead, her attention is diverted and I flex for her. My cock is hard, jerking behind the zipper of my pants and she shivers. Again, another throb, and the beauty steps back.

I let her.

I want her to see the effect she has on me.

My need is palpable. From the very first moment I saw her across the room a few weeks ago, sipping coffee from a Styrofoam cup, I've hungered for this precious girl. It's an uncontrollable yearning I can't control nor do I question it.

She is mine. Always will be.

Every muscle in my body reacts to her lithe form. From the crown of her chestnut hair to her small toes, I take in her body's response while her breathing changes. Fast and panting, her chest falls and rises while two stiff nipples press against the thin cotton of her university shirt.

She's not wearing a bra. Their perkiness doesn't need one.

At once, red-hot fury encases me and I yank her to me again. Jealousy rips through me, I'm angry at anyone who saw her like this. It doesn't matter if it's a male or female; I'm the only person walking this earth allowed to know the shape of her curves.

To know what she smells like. Tastes like.

My obsession knows no bounds and soon enough she'll understand just how deep it runs.

I'm going to own her today and all the tomorrows that follow. Her every breath and sigh.

Every part of her will bear the mark of Silas King.

Chest to abdomen, I bring my hand down to just below her round ass. She trembles in my hold but doesn't ask to be released. There's no fight either. No disgust.

Instead, excitement overpowers her rationality.

There's trepidation in her eyes, yes, and a bit of confusion, but no real fear when I lift her lips to hover over mine. Her breath is my inhale. Her taste is so sweet in the air between us.

I'm going to devour you, bunny.

"What's your name, honey?"

"Willow Caddell."

Truthful and sweet. My girl doesn't lie. Not that I'd give her the chance; I know every last detail of who she is and where she comes from.

"Well, Ms. Caddell, I'm Silas King."

"I know who you are. Everyone at this school does," she says with a low keening sound, tilting her hips minutely in my hold. Willow can't control the action, rubbing against my cock the best she can, while letting out a low moan when it throbs against her denim-covered mound.

A visible shiver runs through her. Her pupils are blown wide.

Goose bumps rise across her skin and she bites down on her bottom lip when I walk us toward a small alcove a few feet away. There's no one in this section of the hall, most students have gone to class, but the few that linger also left in a rush.

Away from me. My reputation.

Willow's back meets the wall a second before I bring a finger to her mouth and tap the bitten lip, she gasps. The flesh is plump and soft; I want to bite her, but don't. Not yet. I've taken a lot of liberties with her today; she's not some easy lay.

My beautiful little virgin isn't like the other women at this school and I respect her too much. I won't let her go, but I'll earn the right to what's mine. A little hard work will only make the fruit so much sweeter.

"Then you know I'm not a man who hides what he is? What he wants?"

"Yes."

"Do you understand what this means, Willow? Why you are here?"

"Not by a long shot." She shakes her head, the fog of lust receding a bit. "I'm confused, yet can't help but—"

"Want my touch." I finish for her and my bunny nods. "That's because your body recognizes mine, even if your head hasn't caught up."

"What does that mean, Silas? I'm not some game."

"No, Willow, you're not." My lips brush against the corner of her mouth. A feather-light touch. "You're everything to me." Another soft peck, on her jaw this time. "My present. My future."

"Silas, I—"

"I'll take it slow and earn your trust, sweetheart, but I'm not letting you go." Not going to beat around the bush. No sense in lying. "This is real."

"We just met." Her response is logical, but no real strength behind it. Not when she gyrates against me again. "I don't know you."

"Doesn't change the reality."

"And what's that?" Willow's flushed cheeks almost make me forget my promise a few seconds ago. I want to corrupt her innocence. Bathe in the proof of her pleasure. "Help me understand."

"You'll become Mrs. King before we graduate."

The End For Now...

I have one more surprise for this world coming 2023!!!

"Closer, sweetness." Neither of us miss the gruffness in my tone, how each syllable rumbles up my chest until it's a low and guttural growl.

"Yes, sir," she whispers low, taking her first step toward me. My eyes traverse her short frame, and devour each piece of bare flesh I discover. Take in the rich, dark brown of her hair, and how each loose curl sweeps, then bounces around her bare shoulders.

This tiny morsel of sin is a natural beauty with wide, doe eyes in a rich cerulean tone.

So expressive. Beautiful.

She reminds me of a fairy tale princess. The kind that every dirty bastard covets and wishes to corrupt.

.

Read SIN today!
Beautiful Sinner Series (Book 1)
Link: books2read.com/sin-sin

I am her rage. She is my goddess.
Together they create what I am: a vengeful animal determined to protect what's mine.

NOW LIVE:
Half Truth's: Then
Buy Link: https://books2read.com/u/bxQQGq
Half Truths Goodreads: https://www.goodreads.com/book/show/
57915697-half-truths

RELEASING: 2/20/23
Half Truth's: Now

Buy Link: https://books2read.com/half-truths-now
Goodreads: https://www.goodreads.com/book/show/62501125-half-truths

Series Order:
Little Lies (Live Now)
Little Mate (Live Now)
Half Truths Duet: Isabella & Xadiel
Omissions: Leo & (Surprise)
TBN: Meera & Tero
TBN: Marcia & Cobra Shifter

BEAUTIFUL SINNER SERIES

Each book is a standalone.

Now Live!
SIN (#1)
COVET (#2):
MINE (#3):
YOURS (#4):
RISQUE #5
OWN #6
MY SINFUL VALENTINE

Beautiful Sinner Spin-Off:
CORRUPT